many levels... its core themes being love, responsibility and perseverance. After reading it, you too will officially join the ranks of all of us 'Goobers' who love, admire and cherish him dearly."

Nina Blackwood,

Television & radio broadcaster/best-selling author and lifelong animal steward

Author Photograph © 2013 Cristy Gravitt

ABOUT THE AUTHOR

Anne Carmichael was born in Lexington, Kentucky, where she resides today.

She attended the University of Kentucky, where she majored in Fine Arts. Anne loves to draw and paint in her spare time. She also maintains a freelance interior design business, which allows her to pursue yet another artistic passion.

Anne's previous literary works include *The Gertrude Ann and Banjo Series*, a collection of children's poetry which were inspired by her son, daughter and grandchildren; a book for teen horse enthusiasts, *Darby at the Derby*; and *Polar Opposites*, which she wrote in conjunction with photographer, Andrew Fore, Ambassador for Polar Bears International.

Anne is currently the executive assistant to the president of a thoroughbred horse farm in the Bluegrass State. She plans to retire in the next few years and pursue her writing career full-time.

MAY I BE FRANK?

Cohesion Press

Australia

This story is purely fictional and does not represent any real persons, animals or events. Magoo is the only exception.

MAY I BE FRANK?

BY

ANNE C. CARMICHAEL

BOOK TWO OF THE MAGOO WHO SERIES

ARTWORK BY

MONTY BORROR & GREG CHAPMAN

Cohesion Press

2014

FIRST EDITION

10 9 8 7 6 5 4 3 2 1

May I Be Frank?

Anne C Carmichael

Layout by Cohesion Editing and Proofreading

Paperback

ISBN-10: 0-9923339-9-7

ISBN-13: 978-0-9923339-9-7

Cohesion Press

www.cohesionpress.com

"No one saves us but ourselves. No one can and no one may.

We ourselves must walk the path." ~Buddha

DEDICATION

'Thank you to all my readers, for helping
me to find my path.'
~Anne Carmichael

THE PUBLISHER WOULD LIKE TO THANK:
Anne Carmichael
Scott Angstadt and Colleen Kelly-Angstadt

For all the support:
♥ Dawn, David, Leah, and Mike ♥

For the great artwork:
Greg Chapman and Montgomery Borror

Last, but certainly never least,
to the readers!

You all rock!

CONTENTS

GUILTY PLEASURES

You thought you could get away from us, dint ya, Frank, ya punk? Look at you, lying here sunning yerself, like you haven't got a care in the world. Well, you're about to join yer Momma," said Snake as he struck the first blow, meant only to make me aware of his presence and the fact that the Southside Brawlers never allowed anyone to escape their vengeance – not even kittens who hadn't done anything more than to have the misfortune to be born in an alley that had been claimed by the gang.

Stunned by the first pounding from Snake's massive foreleg, I shielded my face and looked up at my attacker. "Snake! We haven't done anything to you." Such a thunderbolt of fear ran through my body that I could hardly speak, but I was angry. Angry that I – and my blind brother, Goo – had survived nearly a year of hardships just to reach this. The thought of it all being lost in one foul blow filled me with hatred towards the gang who had killed our mother.

"Momma hadn't done anything to you either," I yelled. "She just needed a safe place to have me and Goo. This is a city park. You don't own it. Now go away and leave us alone!"

"Why, you ballsy little brat! Who do you think yer talkin' to?" said Snake, as he moved in for the kill. A look of sheer evil came over his face as he lunged with what he intended to be a single, fatal bite into my neck.

🐾 🐾 🐾

With blood dripping from his fangs, Snake looked down at Frank and, assuming that he was very near death, turned to the rest of the gang. "Where's the other one? He's got to be here somewhere. Fer heavensake, he's blind. He couldn't have gone too far away from his brother."

"We've looked everywhere, Boss," Shadow lied. He was lazy and the sun was hot and made him squint. He much preferred to take care of business after dark.

Rickets, ever anxious to please the alpha cat

began to stutter. "Yeah Boss. I even w... went all the way up by the p... p... pond. Goo ain't nowhere."

"Yeah, well maybe he didn't make it through the Winter. Let's get outta here. My work here is done," Snake said as he gave Frank's still body a final kick.

🐈 🐈 🐈

I don't remember much about the first week at the clinic. I later learned from some of the older inmates that they had rushed me right in to surgery. They told me that they'd overheard the docs say they had to replace the blood that I'd lost and that it took over hundred stitches to patch me back together.

"Yeah, you were pretty scary lookin'when you came back from surgery. None of us thought you'd make it through the night," said one of eighteen kittens who were housed at the shelter awaiting adoption.

"I never should have let my guard down," I thought, as I listened to my new-found friends at the shelter sharing the bits and pieces of my intake that I couldn't recall. It was foolish to lie there unprotected, right out in daylight. There might as well have been a neon sign pointing the way to me and Goo. Even as Snake's long teeth sank into my throat, my first thought was Goo. I always thought of my brother first. From the moment I realized that he was blind, I had appointed myself his guardian and protector. But that time, I let him down. I left him totally alone on that fateful day, not that I had much choice. I was critically wounded; but even as the beating was taking place, I was listening for Goo. I heard not a sound out of him. I couldn't see. The first few blows from the Southside Brawlers left my eyes swollen shut. The gang had descended on me just as they had our mother when we were just kittens. She had given her life to save me and Goo and I would've done the same for him, but fate stepped in and took it all out of my hands. Two men from Animal Control had rescued me and brought me here to the clinic. I'm sure if Goo had been anywhere nearby, they would've brought him in as well, even if he wasn't hurt. The fact that they didn't led me to assume that Goo was either very well hidden, that his death had been mercifully quick, or that he got away. Wherever he is, I hope that he knows I would never have left him willingly. I guess I owe my life to the people here at the pound."

"Come on now, pal. Don't beat up on yourself. You couldn't help what happened. I've heard about the Brawlers. We all have. You didn't stand a chance. Not a one of us in here could've done any better. I bet your brother got away. You said he's got pretty keen survival senses, on account of him being blind and all. Yep, I bet maybe the same person who called and reported the fight picked him up and took him home with them and he's living the life somewhere right at this very moment," said the calico in the fourth cage from the left.

"I hope you're right," I said. I'm not going to lie – the first few days after I was brought in were rough. I heard them say I had lost over two thirds of my blood. But ya know, even worse is the damage that thug Snake had done to my face. I was always the pretty one. Now, I look worse than Rickets. He's the one of the Brawlers with legs bent like the rim of a sardine can. I caught a glimpse of myself in the shiny glass doors of the cabinets in the infirmary a few days ago. I guess the docs did a fair job of stitching me up, but my face and neck look like a broken zipper. Oh sure, the wounds have healed, but I'll never be the same. Now I stand about as good of a chance of getting adopted as Goo.".

Oh, Goo, I thought. *What must've happened to him by now? I've been in this place for nearly a month. Who am I kiddin'? I know that Snake and the Brawlers went straight for Goo as soon as they finished with me. For all I know they took him out even before I lost consciousness. Without me, poor ole Goo didn't stand a chance. Rest in peace little brother.*

I curled up with my back to the crate door, so that the other animals would think I was napping. In truth, I was deep in thought.

I guess in some ways Goo's better off now. It must've been hard on him, never being able to see what was going on around him. He must've been scared. Wonder if he cried out for me? I can't think about that now. No, I just have to do what I did that fateful day – survive. Gotta take care of *me* for a change. I didn't really mind lookin' out for Goo. Really I didn't. Oh sure, some days it was a drag having to wait on him to catch up; and it was a little embarrassing at times when we were with friends and he would bump into everything. Sometimes he'd knock things over and make all kinds of commotion, but everybody understood that he couldn't help it.

I feel a little guilty sayin' this, but since I've been back on my feet, it's been kind of nice to just lay around and relax and not have to always be thinking about whether Goo has enough to eat or whether he's in a safe place for the night. I mean, I loved my brother – don't get me wrong – but I never really had a life of my own. From the time we left home, I took charge. I stepped up and became Goo's eyes. He never asked me to take care of him though – never even wanted it. Sometimes he even got mad when I tried to help him. Heaven forbid I let on like I saw him stumble and fall! That really made him mad. He'd just keep trying over and over and over until he got it right. Determined. That was the word for Goo. He was a tough little guy. If he'd have made it, I bet he would've been real independent and I bet he would've walked around like he was King of the Streets. But he couldn't have survived. If the Brawlers tore me up this bad, no way my little blind brother would've had a chance. Yeah, he's better off now. Maybe there is an afterlife and he's reunited with our Mom. She's probably taking care of him now.

I kicked back in the cage that was now my home and breathed a sigh of relief. Although I worried a bit about when my time might run out at the shelter, at least I didn't have to scrounge through garbage pails for meals or hold up in run down garages during storms and winter weather. As bad as it sounded, I was relieved to no longer be my brother's keeper.

Just as I was about to curl up for my third nap of the day, a volunteer abruptly threw open the crate. "Buddy boy, your time has come!" said the volunteer as she lifted me into her arms and sped down the hallway through double doors which led into a part of the shelter that I'd never seen before. My mind began racing to the hurried pace of the girl's stride. *'What – where— where are we going? Wait! Where are you taking me?'* I wondered and began to try to claw my way out of her arms.

"Stay strong, little buddy," shouted the Beagle in the far corner.

"It'll be OK. I think you're heading in the

right direction," said the nervous Cocker Spaniel in the crate nearest the hallway.

"Just be calm. Either way, no point in fighting," said the old tortoise cat, that was next on the PTS list for Thursday.

And from the little tiniest of the kittens in the cage next to Frank's now vacated cage, "You were a good friend, Frank. We'll miss you."

I swallowed hard as I rapidly shuffled various scenarios through my mind.

I know that they took in a whole truckload of mongrel dogs from some puppy mill out near the railroad a day or two ago. Lord knows the filthy beasts made enough noise when they arrived at Intake – barked and howled for hours until they were all vetted, fed and deloused. Thank goodness processing seems to take the spit and vinegar out of everybody. I don't recall much about that time myself. I guess they had me sedated throughout the worst of it. But now they have a full house, and from what I've been told, when the place fills up, somebody has to go. Bad news is it's usually the ones who've been here the longest or the ones that just don't stand much of a chance of being adopted. I've been here a month, cost them a bunch of money and with this hacked up mug of mine, ain't nobody going to want to adopt me.

This must be it. My time must be up.

My short life flashed before my eyes. Suddenly, I was back in Marconi Park in Philadelphia. I recalled Luther, the Great Dane, warning me and Goo about the pound (the shelter) and the shot (euthanasia).

Yep. My number is up. I'm on the way to get the shot. Well, I've had my share of needles since I came in. One little prick and it will all be over. They call this place the humane society, so hopefully this ending will be just that – humane. I'll just go to sleep and never wake up.

OK, Goo, Momma, here I come. I'm tired. I'm ready. Let's get this over.

As I lay back in the volunteer's arms awaiting the inevitable, I heard the happy shriek of a small child. I opened my eyes and pulled back. Quickly, a parental figure stopped the child from reaching out for me.

"Lucy! Wait honey. We have to be very, very gentle with the kitty for a while. He's had a very bad accident and he still has some stitches."

While the adults spoke with the shelter staff, the volunteer gently placed me into a transport crate on a soft towel and muttered something about be happy and enjoy your new home. Within a matter of matter minutes, I was loaded into the back seat of a newer model minivan and the child gooed and cooed and stuck her stubby little fingers at me through the wire closure for what seemed like hours. When the vehicle came to a stop, the man who had been driving the van retrieved the crate with me inside and took me into a modest, but comfortable two story brownstone. A soft bed had been prepared for me in the laundry room off the kitchen, and there were bowls of fresh water and food within easy reach.

Can this really be happening? Have I been adopted? Or maybe I got the shot and I've died and gone to Heaven. Nice as it is, I don't see Goo or Momma and I doubt seriously that Heaven would permit this kid to be annoying me. Oh well, what's a little inconvenience when I may have landed the best home I've ever had in my entire life.

I spent the remainder of the week getting used to my new surroundings. I did my best to accommodate the routine that the family had established, but there were a few bumps in the road: for example, they seemed to want me to use a small, plastic pan full of gravel as a toilet.

How barbaric! Do these people have any idea what gravel feels like between your toes? Not happening people. I'll go outside like I've been doing the last two years, thank you very much.

At least give me some nice soft, cottony blue pads like they had at the shelter. Staff had put those pads in my kennel when I was too sick to go outside. When I felt better, they had opened a little door in the kennel that lead to my very own little yard with grass and sky and fresh air. Thank goodness the vet left my claws intact. I might need them to burrow out of this place if they keep making unreasonable demands. And speaking of 'intact'... There is definitely something missing, as I discovered this morning when I was bathing. Well, I suppose I can make a few concessions since I've scored these nice digs, but seriously, I should have been consulted about the removal a vital part of my body!

In the days to come, I was given a clean bill of health by his new veterinarian. The few remaining sutures were removed from my face, neck, and the recently-altered nether regions. Life was good, albeit boring. Yes, my days on the streets had been dangerous and difficult, but at least on the streets, there had been an element of adventure and oh, how I missed adventures. Time after time, I tried to tell my humans how much I craved the outdoors. I even began leaving them little presents by the backdoor, instead of in the litter box. Finally, my plaintive howls were heard and the man installed a pet door. The family had determined that it wasn't realistic to expect a feral street cat to be content living in confinement. The man said that I had been neutered and was up to date on my immunizations, so they decided that allowing me to run free a few hours a day could cause no harm.

How wrong they were.

When I saw the new exit in the back door, I immediately bolted through the rubber opening and inhaled deeply as the first fresh air I'd breathed in weeks wafted past my face. The first few times I ventured outside, I stayed within the boundaries of the tiny green space which the families in this building shared. I investigated the perimeter of the few brick stepping stones, and marked my territory. Finally, I sprung onto the upper bar of the single row of chain link fencing which separated 'my' brownstone from the next building and performed a sort of tightrope act for any and all observers of this demonstration of ownership.

I was unaware that, from a vantage point high up in a chestnut tree across the street, a Maine

Coon cat the size of a fat English Bulldog watched with fiery, orange eyes as I continued my cocky walk around the peripheral of my new world.

The big cat had been named Vincent Van Gato by his owner, an apparent art lover. It stood to reason that she would choose this particular name, because although he stood fifteen inches tall at the shoulder, forty inches in length, and weighed in at a hefty twenty-five pounds, it was apparent that at some point, he had met his match against a worthy opponent and been found lacking, because his right ear was missing.

Regardless of the misfortune that had cost him his ear, the enormity of Vinnie's girth alone was sufficient to hold even the most aggressive cats at bay; add to that his swagger and reputation as the leader of a gang of feline racketeers whose notoriety stretched all the way from Brooklyn to the Midwest, and you had a force with whom few dared to reckon. The irises of Vinnie's eyes were day-glo orange orbs as he lay on one of the more sturdy branches high in the chestnut tree. For the time-being, he would just watch and wait.

When I finally became bored with my solo walk and returned to the comfort of the house via the pet door, Vinnie pounced out of the tree and quickly made his way to share what he had witnessed with the rest of his sinister associates.

A Walk on the Wild Side

Frank's daily routine did not go unnoticed by the don. Vinnie had strategically placed his henchmen on every side of Frank's yard. They knew every move he made and when he could be expected to make that move again.

🐈 🐈 🐈

More and more of my time is spent outside. Even now that temperatures are getting cooler, I want to be outside. You'd think after spending all that time on the streets, I'd want to just cozy-up on a rug and sleep. Makes no sense to me either, but I just can't lie around and do nothing all day and play with balls of yarn and pretend to chase little toy mice. I've gotta get out of here, but I don't want to have to stay out. I guess I want it all. I want to have a place to crash when I'm tired – someplace to come into when it rains or snows. And food – I really like the food here. The family doesn't spend a lot of money on dry food from the store like we had at the shelter: instead, they give me lots of scraps of whatever the lady has cooked for their dinner. It's not like the stuff from the garbage either. It's good and fresh.

What it boils down to is I miss being around my own kind. Oh sure, there's a fluffy girl cat next door who never goes outside. When I'm walking my fence row, I've seen her sitting in her window, sunning. She has a little pink collar with a bell on it and she always raises her pink little nose when I look her way, like she smells something rotten. Fact is, I smell *too* good. The father has discovered he's allergic to cats, but because he doesn't want to break his little girl's heart and get rid of me, he takes medicine and the mother bathes me incessantly. I smell like lavender all the time and a guy should not smell of lavender. It takes me a good two hours of rolling in the dirt and whatever else I can find outside to begin smelling normal again. I guess it's six of one and half dozen of another – the more I roll, the more she bathes me. Adventure – that's what I need. When Goo and I were going through that first tough year, it was scary, but something about even the scary part was exciting. It was a rush to escape getting caught by the skin of our teeth.

Frank strolled out into the yard with his head hung low. *Maybe this pet gig isn't the life for me*, he thought. Maybe I should just run away. Every mess I've gotten into when I was on the streets taught me a valuable lesson. I'm sure if I went back to the streets, I'd be far wiser this time. I know I could survive. On the other hand, I kind of like the family's kid now. Yes, she can be annoying, like the time she'd tried to dress me up in her doll's clothes. She wouldn't be trying that again anytime soon, I wager. I hissed at her and left deep scratches across her legs as I bolted for freedom.

There's got to be a way to keep the family

happy and at the same time make myself happy as well. Maybe if I stay inside during the day and pretend to be the good little kitty for the family, then once they're asleep at night, I can go out on the town. Nothing says I have to be confined inside this yard. There's no fence that tells me I'm supposed to stay in the yard. All I have to do is just walk. That's what I'll do. I'll just take a nice stroll. I need my freedom.

Every night after the family was asleep, Frank hit the pavement. Sometimes he walked until the sun began to come up over the rooftops of the seemingly endless brownstones that lined his street.

This is a pretty nice neighborhood. Oh, there's nothing real fancy about it, but everybody seems pretty cheerful. The streets are lined with big trees, which make the dogs extremely happy, and there are plenty of street lights.

The shopkeepers recognize me now. When I'm heading out for the night, they're usually closing up and going home. There's one guy who works in the local pharmacy that for some reason, doesn't seem too anxious to get home in the evening, I see him come out and lock up. Then he sits on the stoop with his head in his hands, almost as though he's gathering up his courage to face whatever awaits him at home. Maybe he's having problems with the wife. Maybe there's someone there who's sick and he's having a hard time dealing with it. Or maybe there's no one waiting at all and he just hates to be alone. Whatever it is seems to weigh pretty heavily on his mind, so sometimes I'll go over and rub up against his legs and let him pet me. It seems to make him feel better and it feels pretty good to me too.

There's a lady up the way who runs a dress shop. I've been around to the back of the shop and seen another lady in there working on a sewing machine into the wee hours of the morning. The shop stays open a couple of nights a week. I've seen the owner doing all the meet and greets with the customers and she measures them from head to toe. I guess she must give the measurements to the lady in the back who then makes all the clothes for them. The lady who owns the shop is always dressed to the nines. I guess the lady in the back doesn't have time to make herself any new clothes or even repair the ones she has, because she always has on one of the same two flowered shirts and old jeans. One of the shirts has a pocket that's come loose on the top corner. A person's clothes don't have anything to do with who they are inside though. The sewing lady came outside to smoke one night as I was heading home and as tired as she appeared, she still took time to talk to me and pat my head.

The family assumed that something had happened to frighten me when I stopped going outside during the daytime. When I started sleeping all day, they assumed I was sick and they took me to the vet. But of course, I was just tired from long, sleepless nights spent wandering the streets. Having received a clean bill of health, the assumption was that I had just lead a hard life and was merely slowing down and becoming accustomed to my status as house pet. They eventually came to the conclusion that after all I'd been through in just two short years, I deserve to just lay about the house and rest, so they allow me to do just that.

I find it strange that when I take my nightly strolls, I rarely ever see other cats; and yet I feel their presence everywhere I go. Maybe they've heard how tough I am and are afraid to come out. I guess these scars on my face may make it appear that I've been a lot of fights. Ha! Little do they know that I was ambushed and nearly died! Oh well, let them think what they will. I'll just consider that an insurance policy that nobody's going to mess with me again.

Frank's assumption that the other cats were afraid of him was far from the truth, although his scarred face had not gone unnoticed and there was some truth to the perception that he was a fighter. Vinnie decided to find out if his assessment of Frank as a potential partner in crime was on target.

🐈 🐈 🐈

There was a new moon, so it was particularly dark outside. I had strolled up to the Flushing Street Station.

I passed the Price Mart where some older kids were kicking around a deflated soccer ball and talking about things kids of any age shouldn't have to know. For that matter, they shouldn't even be on the streets at this time of night, but when one of them decided it might be fun to torture a cat, I high-tailed it out of there. They chased after me, but a couple of police cars were leaving the 109th Precinct lot as I zipped past, and the kids tried to play it off and casually headed back the other way. There must be a curfew, because I looked back and saw the cops pull over and talk to the boys, who quickly dispersed and, I assume, headed to their respective homes. I tip my hat to New York's finest.

Part of me still wanted to hop on the train and ride into the city and disappear among the crowds. I could be in Herald Square in 30 minutes. I'd always wanted to see NYC. As I sat under a bench hoping to remain obscure, a giant beast of a cat jumped up on top of the bench and peered down through the slats at me. I crouched back against the cement block which prevented the bench from being moved in hopes that he would see that I was no threat. I hoped that he would just go on about his business; but that was not meant to be. It became more and more clear that this guy knew exactly who I was and that he had followed me to the station with some sort of agenda.

"You're called Frank? Well I'll call you Frankie.

That's OK witchu ain't it?" he said without need of a reply, for it became immediately apparent that he already knew pretty much all there was to know about me. Besides, I could tell that he always had things *his* way. How he knew my life story would become clear as the weeks passed. "I hear you're from Philly – the Southside. Heard you got into a bit of a scuffle with the Brawlers over there. Heard you were stickin' up for your brother who was deaf or cripple or somethin'. Family's everything, ain't it kid? Well, I can use a man like you in my organization. Why don't you and me get some food and take a leisurely little stroll across the bridge? Oh, by the way, Vincent is my name, but you can call me Vinnie – all my friends do."

I tried not to appear shaken by this gargantuan feline and hoped that my wobbly legs wouldn't betray me. It wasn't just Vinnie's size that intimidated; it was his swagger-- his sense of ownership of everything and everyone around him. I'd never felt so insignificant in my life. Not even when I was a kitten did I feel so threatened by another animal. Why, even ole Luther, as big as he was, didn't make me feel the way Vinnie did – but then, Luther had a heart of gold. I was pretty sure if, in fact, Vinnie even had a heart, it was hard as stone and as black as coal. I knew I should try to end this one-sided conversation and beat a path back home. When I got there, I would putty up the hole in the pet door and stay inside and count my blessings for the rest of my days. I could tell by his demeanor that no one walks away from Vinnie and lives to tell about it, and as we walked he detailed how I was to fit into his organization.

"Maybe you've heard something about me around town, kid? Well, it's true," Vinnie said, laughing at his own lame joke. Seeming to notice that his comment didn't elicit as much as chuckle from Frank, he continued his sales pitch.

"OK, so maybe I ain't a squeaky clean momma's boy, but me and my boys don't hurt nobody [looking guiltier with every word spoken]. "Well, least not anybody that don't need hurtin'. We take up for our own kind. If youse was to join my little family, that would be like havin' a real good insurance policy, son. Ain't nothing gonna happen to you as long as you're on Vinnie's payroll. We live the Good

Life," he said with a rub of his gelatinous belly, then running his slimy hand across Frank's whiskers. "I can tell from the looks of ya that youse been around the block a time or two."

Obviously, Vinnie had me figured all wrong, but to deny that I was the pugnacious hoodlum he perceived me to be would likely have been a death sentence. If only he knew the feeling of panic that caused a spasm of fright to run down my spine every time he placed his hand on my shoulder and called me 'son'. I hadn't a clue who my father was, but I knew Momma would never have associated with someone like Vincent Van Gato.

As we stood on the pedestrian walkway of the Brooklyn Bridge, I wasn't certain if the swaying motion was from the traffic crossing the suspension bridge or if it was the quivering of my own body which threatened to send me tumbling into the East River. As I leaned against the abutment below the bronze plaque on the tower, I realized that we'd been standing there 'talking' for hours, because the sun was beginning to rise over Manhattan.

Vinnie had tried to convince me that I would

make a name for myself by becoming one of his boys. He talked about how every cat in every state between the Jersey shore and the Mississippi River would know my name and respect me. Whatever my little heart desired could be mine, Vinnie assured me. Even though I wanted to believe that life could be the way Mr. Van Gato was painting it, a part of me kept saying *'run... run fast and never look back'*. But instead, I quickly informed the boss (because at some point during the long night, Vincent Van Gato had made me an offer I couldn't refuse and I was now his employee) that if I was to play this charade well, I had to be back in my home and resume my role as the unassuming house cat. Another atta-boy from Mr. Van Gato and off I scurried to my bed for some much needed sleep before I started my first night on *the job*.

THE INITIATION

I was told to be at an abandoned building over on Flushing at exactly 7:15. I realized that the likely reason for a meeting to be called on the quarter hour was to test my promptness and my ability to follow orders. I also knew that tardiness would not be tolerated, so at precisely 7:15, I climbed through a tangle of mesh chicken-wire that covered a broken window. The chicken-wire seemed designed to keep vagrants from entering the condemned site, but the wire had been peeled back and the pungent odor of urine swirling through the air told me that I was not the first to enter the building.

Humans assume that cats can see well in pitch darkness. Well, let me go on record as saying that assumption is false. When I entered the building, there was not as much as a flicker from a star to guide me. I stumbled and bumbled my way through the room out into a hallway. I called upon my other senses to give me a clue as to which way to go next. The odor of cigarette smoke, cheap beer and urine left by previous tenants (or more likely transients) was all that was detectable to my keen sense of smell. I stood as still as a mouse. Where did that saying originate anyway? In my experience, mice seldom, if ever, remain still! I heard a thud on the floor above and someone shushing whoever had stumbled and made the telling noise. I made my way to the stair railing and began my ascent toward where I believed the sound had originated.

When I reached the top of the stairs, I stopped again to see if I could detect any additional movement which might guide me. What I heard was a whispered argument between two toms.

"You bonehead. Be quiet. Mr. V said the whole point of this little exercise is to see if the new guy is a-skeered to come into an empty building in the dark!"

"Well I can't see squat in the dark. Besides, he ain't here yet like he was 'posed to be. I bet he don't come at all."

"Shhhh. Lower yer voice, you idiot. Maybe he's just a little smarter than you and is just bein' real quiet."

"I can't help it. I swear I think I cut one of the toes on my back foot clean off on that blasted piano wire!"

As I moved nearer the voices, I was able to discern that the argument began when one of them had blown their cover by tripping over the piano wire which had been strung across the bottom of the doorframe with the intent of causing me to fall when I entered the room.

Never one to miss a golden opportunity, I inched my way toward the doorway, using the sound of bickering as my radar.

With the stealth of a ninja, I edged my body along the wall toward the doorway. Then, I slid down the door facing until my paw found the piano wire, which by now I knew had, with the skill of a surgeon, removed the retractile hind claw of the cat who'd tripped over his own booby trap. I struggled not to chuckle at his misfortune.

As the two thugs continued to alternate between fighting and shushing each other, I continued to inch ever closer, until my front paw detected a table leg. I stood almost shoulder to shoulder with the oblivious idiots when I began to emit a low, unwavering growl. Immediately, one of them shone a flashlight in my face and just as suddenly, let out a terrified scream. With my presence known, I quietly began to speak.

"Boys, I believe we had a meeting at precisely quarter-past seven. It is now half-past, and I've been standing here for ten minutes, listening to the two of you acting like schoolboys and wasting my time. Now that I have quite obviously aced Mr. V's initiation exam, can we move this along and get down to business? I'd like to get home before dawn and get in a straight eight before my next assignment."

Ha! Those two clowns stuttered and stammered and tried unsuccessfully to regain their composure, but in the end, all they could manage was to fake a laugh and tell me that I'd done okay and that I should just go home and get my beauty sleep. Someone would get a message to me as to what Mr. V required of me.

IN HARM'S WAY

I was pretty proud of myself when I returned home following my admission into the good ole boys club. And to think, I'd almost chickened out. I don't mind telling you that I had been more than a little intimidated by Vinnie upon our first introduction. Aside from his slimy, potbellied appearance, I knew that he could pound me into mincemeat if he so desired. Vinnie is four times the size of Snake and I'll carry the marks that Snake left on me the rest of my life. But beyond that, I've done a little investigating, and Vinnie's reputation is known all the way up to New England, down to the Ohio Valley and all the way back to South Philly. He's a powerful force that no one (not cat, nor dog, nor even man) would dare to cross.

When I decided to check references on Vinnie,

so to speak, I didn't know who I could trust. I hadn't really made any acquaintances on the street, so I didn't know who might be an associate of his, who his enemies are, who his friends are and who had pledged their loyalty to him. One day, I saw Giselle (that pretty Angora next door) sitting in her usual spot in the window, so I jumped up on the outside ledge and signalled that I'd like to talk to her. She motioned for me to come around to the back door. I discovered that she didn't have a pet door, but she pointed towards the wooden deck at the back of the house and I immediately found a hole that went all the way through to the subflooring. There was a tunnel which had been dug all the way up into the enclosed sun porch where Giselle stood waiting. As I was later to learn, the entire tunnel had been dug by an enthusiastic Labrador Retriever puppy who belonged to the previous owners. Giselle's humans had discussed having the 'tunnel' repaired, but winter had set in before they could locate a repairman, so they'd merely stuffed some old towels into the hole, which with a little help from Giselle, I quickly discarded.

Having never encountered Giselle's humans, I figured I didn't have much time for pleasantries and I cut right to the chase.

"Giselle, I've got a bit of a dilemma and I'm not sure what to do. I take it you've been around these parts for awhile and I thought maybe you could shed a little light on someone I met recently. Have you ever heard of a guy by the name of Vincent Van Gato?"

The look of terror on her face said it all. I didn't really need to or want to know anymore, and yet I persevered. When she had regained her composure, Giselle began to share a painful story with me about her beloved brother, Nicolai's association with Vincent Van Gato. She bowed her head and spoke in reverent tones

"Nicky and I were just eight weeks old when our human, an artist, brought his young wife to live in the Williamsburg neighborhood of Brooklyn. The artist gave us to his wife as a birthday present, shortly after they were married. Whereas I am solid white, my brother was black as midnight. The lady named me Giselle and my brother Nicolai, as a nod to her European heritage.

Because of her upbringing as a naturalist,

the wife felt that all animals – human or otherwise, should be exposed to fresh air at every opportunity, even when the weather was inclement. She chose to hang her laundry outdoors on a clothesline where the all-natural fabrics could absorb the clean scent of a spring or summer breeze. As she hung the laundry on the line, Nicky and I would frolic in the laundry basket. When she went on walks in the rain, we would often snuggle inside the large, interior pockets of her warm parka. Early that first summer, her husband brought home a white wicker basket which he mounted on the handlebars of her bicycle, so that we could ride with her to the farmer's market. We loved those little outings and we adored each other." As Giselle reminisced her voice began to waver and she fought back tears.

I waited as Giselle again tried to gather her thoughts and put my paw on hers to offer comfort. Finally, she continued.

"As we quickly outgrew the baskets and the lady's pockets, she began to allow us more freedom. She'd taught us from a very young age to walk beside or behind her by carrying delectable little morsels of herring or bits of chicken left over from the previous night's dinner in a paper bag, so that the scent would hold our attention. Eventually no treats were required. We never ventured off – until one day in our second season when the man and woman took us for a picnic in the park. We were lying in the sunshine on a gingham patchwork quilt napping while the man and woman took a stroll around the lake. They had left us unattended in this park before and always without incident. Everyone kept their dogs leashed, as was the park rule, and we had never felt the need to wander off and explore," said Giselle with widening eyes as though she were reliving a tale that still evoked nightmares.

"I was always content to find the best sunbeam and bathe in its rays for hours. Nicky, however, had matured into a typical male tom with wanderlust. We had been altered, but Nicky had never lost the need for adventure; and so, when he saw a group of other toms roughhousing in the sand on the volleyball court, he left me sleeping while he went to investigate. As he quickly discovered, this was no mere group of young toms roughhousing; this was a vicious gang of older males vying for territorial rights. Before he could turn and run back to the safety of his family, Nicky was pulled into the fight-till-the-death power struggle. There were two men playing tennis nearby who rushed to break up the fight. One of them turned on the water hydrant, which thankfully sent the other toms running.

One of the men picked Nicky up and I could see that his fur was badly ruffled and there was

blood matted in his beautiful black coat. He looked limp and lifeless. The other man was running from place to place asking people if they were the owners of a black cat. When he reached our owners, they immediately picked me up and grabbed our belongings and rushed Nicky to the Emergency Pet Clinic. Thankfully, his wounds were all superficial and he was cleaned up, treated and released. His physical wounds healed in a few days, but the emotional scars never did. Nicky vowed that he would never lose another fight. His personality changed. He was bitter and angry. He was determined to show the world that he was in control of not only himself, but all those around him. His search for power lead him right to Vincent Van Gato's door. "

I thought the story ended there, because Giselle sighed and collapsed on a nearby braided yarn rug. But in a moment, she took yet another cleansing breath and continued her story, as though it was somehow cathartic. Perhaps she was relieved to have someone with whom she felt she could share her burden.

"Van Gato's *modus operandi* had always been to take young, strong, angry toms and make them stronger and angrier and yet dependent upon him in some way. All it took to recruit Nicolai into the Van Gato 'family' was to assure him that I would be protected for life. Beyond that, Nicky gave no thought for his own safety or reputation. He would do anything at Vinnie's bidding, even if it ultimately meant giving his life on orders from his deranged mentor. And that is exactly how Nicky's life ended one cold, October evening.

It was All Hallows Eve (Halloween). Vinnie had a score to settle with a small-time hood over in Flatbush. Under the guise of the neighborhood's Halloween festivities, Nicky was to buddy up to the scroungy tom, convince him to masquerade as the proverbial witch's black cat by spray painting him and then lure him into a dark parking lot behind a local bar, where the rest of Vinnie's thugs lay in wait. All went according to Vinnie's sinister plan. At precisely midnight, Nicky and his victim arrived at the appointed location. But the other gang members mistook Nicky's black coat for that of the intended victim and by the time Vinnie arrived to claim his victory, Nicky had breathed his last breath. Without the least compunction or remorse, Vinnie had Nicky's corpse tossed into the nearby dumpster and ordered that his name never be spoken again. However, due to a certain convoluted code of ethics among gangsters, Vinnie also decreed that I was to be guarded and protected by the mob for the remainder of my days.

As I listened to Giselle's retelling of the story of her brother's death and his association with

Vincent Van Gato, the only words which I heard were 'power', 'loyalty', and 'conviction'. Yes, this was what I'd been looking for – I wanted the power. I wanted a 'family' that would have my back and I would have theirs. I was ready to take whatever oath was required.

Rung by Rung

I've clawed my way up the ladder in Vincent Van Gato's organization. I'm his personal associate now. Vinnie doesn't make a move without me, but it hasn't always been that way. I had to earn his trust. I started out with silly little gigs, but I realize now, they were mean and wrong. Even at the time, my conscience gnawed at me. For example, there was my first job at the market.

That first heist was perpetrated on an old lady who frequented the local Pick and Save Market. When I say frequented, I mean she shopped there every single day, come rain or shine, spring, summer, fall and winter at exactly 10am. I don't know why she didn't shop once a week like most people. Maybe it was because she only had so much room in that little carry-all of hers. Maybe she didn't have room in her tiny little kitchen to store more. Maybe it was because she didn't have the money. Maybe she liked to get out of the house. Whatever the reason, you could set your watch by her. The only variance was what she purchased on each day of the week. On Monday mornings, she always got a big piece of meat and a whole fish – enough to build meals around for the entire week. On the first Monday morning of the month, she paid for her groceries with a check sent to her by her hot-shot son who lived over in the city. There was always money left over to last her the rest of the month, so the grocer would give her cash back.

We'd been watching the store for a couple of weeks. The grocer arrived every morning at 6am. First, he would put on an old apron that he kept on a hook by the side door. Then he would sweep and mop the floors until they shined like a new penny. By 7am, the delivery boy from the meat market would deliver packages of fresh meat. From my vantage point on a nearby rooftop, I could see packages marked as steaks, rib roast, chuck roast, ground beef, turkey, and chicken. It's a wonder he didn't hear my belly rumbling as I made mental note of his schedule and tracked his every move.

Soon after the meat was delivered, the guy would arrive from the seaport with the Catch of the Day. That was almost more than I could stand. More than once, I thought about just knocking off the fish truck, but then the jig would've been up and blow our whole operation.

Next to arrive was the green grocer with fruits and vegetables. Every morning at 8am, the grocer filled the crates out in front of the market with the produce he brought. One time, after the grocer discarded the carrying crates out back, I saw that one of the wooden crates had landed beneath the steps. It was lined with a piece of brown paper to protect the lettuce from being crushed. It reminded me of the place where Goo and I were born outside the Deli. It reminded me of Cook. It reminded me of Momma. I got a little choked up, so I quickly put it out of my mind. I had to toughen up. Gangsters don't cry!

On the first Monday of the following month, I watched as the grocer went through his morning agenda. His schedule had never varied once in his thirty years as the proprietor. The delivery men came and went and at precisely 10am, along came the little old lady dragging her shopping cart behind her. I watched as she filled her cart with a beautifully marbled rump roast that looked too big for a lady her size to eat in a month, let alone a week. Next, she reached into a tray of ice and lifted out a red snapper. The grocer lifted it into the hanging scale for her. It weighed nearly two pounds! He wrapped the two pieces of meat in white paper and then placed the parcels into an insulated bag to keep it fresh. After selecting several fresh vegetables, some herbs, a carton of berries and some fresh cream, the old lady stepped up to the cash register to pay for her groceries. As he did every month, the grocer gave her a handful of bills and some coins in return. They exchanged pleasantries and he held the door for her as she dragged her carry-all onto the sidewalk. It was show time.

I waited until the lady pulled the cart past the watchful eye of the grocer, who then turned to assist other shoppers. I signalled to my partner and then pounced from the rooftop and ran under the old lady's feet, causing her to tip the cart and spill the contents onto the pavement. My accomplice grabbed the snapper while I returned to grab the roast. We made off as quickly as we could, given the weight of the load we were carrying.

When we got back to headquarters, Vinnie and the others were waiting to assess the haul. I was out of breath and my legs wouldn't stop shaking as I threw the roast down on the table for Vinnie's approval. I thought he'd be pleased with such a feast, but he remained silent and emotionless as he told the boys to divide up the food. It wasn't like Vinnie *needed* anything. He had the food of kings at home. He wanted for nothing. These little pranks were strictly for his amusement and to make a name for himself. They were also a testing ground to evaluate the skills of those who did his bidding. Succeeding in this mission didn't make me feel particularly brave or skilful. In fact, the last thing in the world I wanted for dinner was that little lady's food.-

DUPLICITY

My plans to sleep all day and work all night were unravelling. My humans had become overly concerned about my sleeping all the time. For all they knew, I never left my bed. They, of course, had no idea that I went out as soon as they fell asleep and most days, I barely got back home before they woke to begin their day.

I bet they took me to the vet five times. He performed every test known to man on me. He did blood work to see if I was low on iron or if I had some viral disease. He checked me for worms – twice! He put me under some machine and made pictures of my insides. Since the tests showed nothing wrong (because of course, there was nothing wrong that a few hours sleep wouldn't fix), he thought I might not be getting enough vitamins, so every morning, the mother would wake me up to give me a pill big enough to choke a horse. I've got to admit, the vitamins did give me more stamina to perform the jobs that Vinnie lined up for me.

I overheard the humans talking one morning over breakfast. The mother said maybe I was just depressed and needed a change. She thought maybe since I'd been on my own for so long before my accident, that I'd be happier on a farm someplace in upstate New York where I could be a barn cat and help keep the mouse population down. My first thought on hearing that lame plan was, No! Oh for god's sake, woman, never, ever make me go back to living on disgusting rodents again! City living with you people may not be a walk in the park, but the food is plentiful, the bed is soft and warm and, except for that kid always trying to play her silly games with me, it's not a bad place. Certainly nowhere near as bad as where I've been. I knew that I had to come up with a plan and fast!

Since the whole issue seemed to be that the family thought I was sleeping 'round the clock and since I knew that I couldn't function without a minimum of a straight eight, and since Vinnie's jobs were all after dark, for obvious reasons, I decided that maybe I needed to just appreciate the soft life I'd been given as a house pet and stop burning the candle at both ends. I went to Vinnie to discuss my dilemma.

"Vinnie, I've run into some problems at home. Since the family doesn't realize that I'm not safely tucked into my bed all night and they see me sleeping all day, they think I must be sick or something. They've had me to the vet more times than I can count, and let me tell you, that's no walk in the park! Do you have any idea what they do to you when they don't have much to go on? Well, let me tell you, it's downright invasive. I realized that I was rambling, but I was nervous and couldn't seem to stop myself. "I really appreciate the great opportunity you've given me, but I'm afraid I'm just going to have to resign."

I thought Vinnie was going to blow a gasket when I said that.

"Oh you do, do you?" he said. "Did you type up a nice little resignation letter for me and everything? Hmmm? Well ain't this just a fine kettle of fish. Boy, nobody quits the organization – *ever*. The only way you leave the Van Gato family is in a pine box."

I realized then that I knew too much already. I belonged to Vincent Van Gato.

After he calmed down, Vinnie suggested that I do some morning jobs for him and I agreed to start small and see if worked out. Of course, one way or another, I knew that if something had to go, it would be my home life. Clearly, no one quits Vinnie.

On a good day, Vinnie has mood swings. On a bad day, he has the whole playground. Fortunately for me, that day was a good day, He quickly flip-flopped and invited me to stay for brunch. I didn't hang around to eat. I had food waiting for me at home. There is always plenty to eat at home. I think in the beginning the vet told the family to keep my food and water bowls full at all times, so that I would put on some weight. I don't need to gain any more weight now, but they always keep my food bowls full. I appreciate that.

When I arrived back at the house later that morning, I found Lucy sitting on the couch watching TV. She was holding her favorite doll and shivering under a blanket. I knew she should've been at school. Her mother came in carrying a tray with some dry toast and juice for her, but Lucy just shook her head and lay back down on the sofa. She was all sweaty and pale. Next thing I knew, she picked me up and shoved me under the blanket with her and as soon as I stopped trying to get free, the kid fell asleep. I didn't want to wake her, seeing as how she was sick and all, so I just curled up on the blanket and tried to go to sleep. I used to fall asleep at the drop of a hat, but now, even though I'm always dead tired at the end of my shift, I do a lot of tossing and turning and thinking.

As I lay there, my mind wandered back to

the old lady whose groceries we'd stolen when I first went to work for Vinnie. In my mind's eye I could still see her lying on the sidewalk, so tiny—no more than five feet tall, and so thin that her frame looked like one of the branches on a young redbud tree that could snap if you brushed up against it. I really hope she wasn't hurt. I'd thought about going back around the store to see if I could find out anything about her, but the guys would've thought I was soft, so I never did.

Finally, my memories and my conscience allowed me to fall asleep, but Lucy was restless from fever, so I quietly extricated myself from her arms and went back to the laundry room to my own bed.

IT AIN'T PERSONAL - IT'S BUSINESS

Conscience has no place in my line of work. It just gums up the process and keeps you from getting a straight eight. After the first half dozen jobs, I toughened up. I used to think about that first old lady all the time. I admit it did bother me some when I heard that she broke a hip in the fall that day and ended up in a nursing home because her ingrate kids (the son, a big shot lawyer over in Manhattan and the daughter, some fancy decorator in Connecticut) were too busy with their careers to take care of her. Seems to me the least they could've done would have been to hire somebody for her so she could stay in her own place, but that's no concern of mine. Serves 'em right that me and my boy ran off with the meal she was supposed to cook for them that day.

I guess I played it the way Vinnie wanted because he kept giving me more responsibility. We can wreak some havoc. Gets the ole adrenaline pumping to know that any moment you could get caught and hauled off to the pound. Lord help me, I never want to go there again! But this gig keeps me entertained and I can swap hats and go home and play sweet, fluffy kitty cat anytime I want. Best of both worlds, ya know? Only thing is, it's not just fun and games anymore.

When I got into the business, it was just pinch some food or retribution for some perceived wrong that had been perpetrated on Vinnie. One time, there was this chef at a fancy restaurant who had pissed Vinnie off. We waited until the guy from the Health Department came to inspect the place, and then I went down into the sewers and chased a whole slew of rats up through the air ducts. They were dropping out of the ceiling into pots of soup and on the fancy silver serving trays – it was great. Shut the restaurant down for thirty days!

But now Vinnie has promoted me to his right-hand man and I'm learning the full scope

of the business. It's not just pranks anymore. Vinnie calls it 'Public Service Work'. When I first met him, I was intimidated by him and I thought he must be the most powerful cat in all of New York. But then once I started doing the prankin', it just seemed like he was full of hot air because the only real danger in what we were doing was maybe getting swatted with a broom and shooed away. If anybody had been quick enough to catch us (which they weren't), they would've just thrown us back out in the street.

So what, right? Well, in my new position I go do jobs with Vinnie alone. He doesn't trust nobody else. He tells me *everything* and, if I'm being honest I have to tell you, '*everything*' is scaring the bejezzus out of me.

I guess I should be pleased that I've climbed to the top of organizational ladder, so to speak, but it's a heavy burden to carry, especially when you don't have friends for support. I've never quite fit in with the rest of Vinnie's men. Me and Johnny used to be pretty tight, but that was back when Johnny was Vinnie's second in command. The more responsibility that Vinnie gives me, the more he takes away from Johnny. I've tried to let Johnny know that I didn't ask for, nor do I want, this place in the Van Gato hierarchy. Johnny said he understood and that it's all in what Vinnie wants and what Vinnie wants, Vinnie gets; but it's pretty apparent that it's not sitting well with Johnny. Not sitting well at all. In fact, I'm beginning to feel the need to watch my back where Johnny is concerned.

Take, for example, just last week. Vinnie heard that there was a gang of no account petty thieves over in Detroit. *Detroit*, I say. That's probably more than a hundred miles from Brooklyn, but Vinnie hears stuff from all over. Anyhow, this gang calls themselves The Motocats – has something to do with Detroit being the Motor City or something. Anyway, these Motocats were just small time – doing pranks like my boys and I used to do, but then somewhere along the line, they got mean. They wouldn't just break stuff and steal; they took to hurting people bad and killing other animals. When word got to Vinnie what they were doing, he told me we were going to Detroit. When Johnny heard that Vinnie was taking me to Detroit to do a job instead of him, he acted real weird towards me. Started calling me Vinnie Junior and saying 'Yes sir' and saluting me every time I said anything to him. I came right out and asked him if he had a problem.

"Why, no sir, I don't have any problems. None at all, sir. Can I help you pack a bag, sir?" And as he walked away, I heard him mutter, "Ya little weasel..."

Oh well, I didn't have time to focus on Johnny and his petty jealousy. The boss was ready to leave for Detroit.

Like I said, Detroit was a long way from New York. We had to go to the bus station and hop into the storage area underneath the bus going to Detroit and stay in there for a day and a half! The fumes from the diesel fuel alone were enough to choke a mule. I got sick twice in somebody's suitcase. Only good thing was we were so sick from the fumes that we didn't think about food at all.

Well, we asked around and found out where The Motocats hung out and we sat outside their digs until a cat that looked to be the leader came

out. He was laughing and picking his green, furry teeth with a splintered piece of wood. But when he saw Vinnie, he stopped dead in his tracks. Vinnie whispered to me to butch up. I think I do look tougher now, 'cause most of the other cats and even some of the dogs at home stutter and shake like a leaf when I come around.

Vinnie got all up in the cat's face and I stood between them and the other Motocats and looked as tough as I could manage. The big one tried to act all bad and asked Vinnie what he was doing out of New York. Vinnie told him that in case he hadn't heard, his territory ran all the way up the East Coast, down to Atlanta and across the Midwest. He said he even has connections in California. I didn't know that, but if Vinnie said it, it must be true. Vinnie said that he'd heard rumors that The Motocats had been attacking people and killing their own kind. The whole time he was talking, Vinnie kind of slapped the big guy on the jowls and tweaked his nose. The punk grabbed Vinnie's paw and pushed him away. I could've told him that was a very wrong thing to do, but by then Vinnie had him by the neck and had dug his claws in so deep the blood was dripping out of the puncture wounds.

"Now, I'm going to just assume that these rumors which made it all the way from Detroit to New York are false and I won't hear anything of the sort ever again, will I?" says Vinnie. And the ole boy just shook his head real gentle-like because Vinnie's claws were still dug in deep. I glanced down at the sidewalk and saw that Mr. Big Shot had wet himself. His boys had also noticed that he was standing in a puddle of his own pee and I reckon that was sufficient to make him look less like a leader because they just shook their heads and walked away.

Me and Vinnie found something to eat and then climbed in the first bus back to New York. On the one hand, I respected Vinnie for making the head of the Motocat gang stop hurting people and killing animals. But on the other hand, I realized just how far Vinnie's authority stretched and I was afraid of what he might ask me to do next. Add to that Johnny's new attitude and I had more than enough to keep me up nights.

At least I knew to watch my back where he was concerned. Seemed Johnny also needed to figure out who he could and couldn't trust. Mike, another of Vinnie's boys met us at the bus station. He told Vinnie that he'd just come to greet us and see if there was anything we needed; but as soon as Vinnie was out of earshot, Mike told me that Johnny had been acting like King of the Mountain in Vinnie's absence and that he'd been bad-mouthing me to everybody who would listen. I was definitely going to have to have an in-depth discussion with Johnny when the time was right. But I had learned yet another valuable lesson on that trip. I learned that there was a code, even among criminals. I would soon find out that I needed to study the code book more carefully the day I got my next assignment.

ALWAYS READ THE FINE PRINT

If ever there was a career for which there should be a detailed job description and a printed training manual to which one might refer when questions arise regarding a particular procedure, it is mine. There should also be a Contract for New Hires which outlines every possible scenario one might encounter on the job and the expectations of how the employee must perform in each instance. If such a contract had existed and had I read the fine print, I might have given a second and perhaps even a third thought to my career path. Instead, my training had been on the job. The method was 'fly-by-the-seat-of-my-pants'. Oh, and one more thing – the employer should definitely provide ample life insurance!

Don't get me wrong, I'm not getting cold feet. I'm still an adrenaline junkie. It's just that sometimes I ask myself what is all for? I mean, in the case of the gang in Detroit, I think we might have made a difference. We likely put the fear of God in their low-life operation and maybe they'll cease and desist. But overall, I don't see that we're implementing change. In fact, we start as much trouble as we eliminate. Maybe I'm just tired. It's all academic anyhow. Like Vinnie says, you don't resign from this job. Maybe you *are* allowed vacation, though. I think I'll check into that. But before I could submit a request for time off, Vinnie sent me an urgent message

I should really talk to Vinnie about sending messages via Johnny, because I didn't know if either of us could trust him anymore. But Johnny had been in the organization for many years and talking about him in derogatory terms to Vinnie might turn around and bite me on the tail, so I just listened to what Johnny had to tell me and took mental notes that I'd best double check everything he said before I walked into a hornet's nest.

May I Be Frank

"Vinnie says you're to meet your contact at the construction site at Pier 6 in Brooklyn Bridge Park," Johnny told me. "He says you're to appear unobtrusive (whatever that means) and blend in. He says the contact has been briefed on your background and he has a photo of you. He was an old friend of Vinnie's family and you're to assist him in every way possible. That was the extent of it. Oh, and good luck, buddy boy. You're gonna need it," said Johnny with a smirk.

At the appointed time, just as the sun was beginning to set on the water, I sat perched on the top of a bench by the waterfront and waited. I'd been there only a few minutes when the contact arrived and jumped up beside me. He

looked straight ahead at the water and spoke in low tones, as though he was merely asking the time of day as he gazed out at a tugboat moving slowly on the horizon. He identified himself only as Mr. Smith. When he finished giving me instructions, he hopped off the bench and casually went on his way, as though he had briefly stopped for a rest and was now just moseying on back from whence he came.

When Mr. Smith left the pier, I sat absorbing all that he had said. I didn't like the feel of this job and I didn't like Mr. Smith. He wouldn't even give me his real name. I hoped that Vinnie was unaware of the details of this assignment, because I would feel betrayed if I thought he had knowingly put me in a position where I wasn't being given all the facts and with a guy who might not have my back if things should go wrong. I needed to know that Vinnie would support my decision if I decided not to comply with Mr. Smith's request.

Although I needed to get home and at least make an appearance before the night shift, I was compelled to go on up to Vinnie's place in the city and get his take on this assignment. When

May I Be Frank

I got to Vinnie's place, Johnny, was sitting on the pedestal of a marble lion that adorns the entrance of the Park Avenue townhouse that Vinnie calls home.

This 22,000 square foot, three story apartment is owned by the wealthy young widow of a

shipping magnate that Vinnie cajoled into taking him in and treating him in the manner to which he hoped to become accustomed. Ha! He surely has become accustomed to this way of life – Vinnie is treated as royalty. The doorman holds the door for him, as though he was the master of the mansion. He has his own suite, complete with a kitty king velvet bed, a customized litter box that flushes automatically in his personal *ensuite* bathroom, and a closet full of custom-made designer pet clothes. The woman has even installed a kitchenette in the suite, stocked with all of Vinnie's favorite foods, which includes Almas caviar (£800 for those on a budget or £16,000 if you prefer the 24-karat gold container) and of course, he must have Bling H_2O (forty bucks a bottle, with Swarovski crystals encrusted on the frosted glass). He has filet mignon at least three nights a week. No wonder he had bladder crystals removed last year and spent two weeks at the Park Avenue Pet Clinic.

I was physically exhausted from the long hike from my neighborhood to Brooklyn Bridge Park. I had managed to slip down into the subway and onto a train into the city, but then I missed my connection and had to hoof it all the way from the West End to Central Park and on over to Park Avenue. I soon became mentally exhausted as well when I finally reached Vinnie's place only to have Johnny tell me that the Missus had taken Vinnie out to the Hamptons for the weekend. She thought he needed a rest. Right. I was doing all the work and *he* needed a rest.

The thought crossed my mind that with Vinnie out of town, I could just bail out on Mr. Smith's little project and say that there were problems Before the thought had time to even gel in my mind, it was interrupted by the rest of the message from the Boss.

"Vinnie thought that you might not take to Mr. Smith. He said you'd come here after you met with him. He said when you did come running up here, to tell you that you was to do whatever Mr. Smith needed you to do. That was a direct order. When he gets back from his long weekend of rest, he expects the mission to be completed Do you understand?" Johnny said. He loved relaying orders. It made him feel like a big shot.

There was no point in going home. I was supposed to meet Mr. Smith's associate at midnight near the carousel in Central Park. The only saving grace to this day was that Johnny had access to Vinnie's amazing suite.

As it did on many an occasion, Johnny's personality flip-flopped back to compadre and he poked me in the ribs and invited me up to the suite until it was time to head back to work. Vinnie always gave Johnny permission to use the suite when he, the Missus, and all the household staff were away. It did require shimmying up the drain pipe, but nevertheless, Vinnie had unlocked the French doors, just as he promised.

"Come on, Frankie. You ain't got nothin' better to do than live like royalty for a few hours, do ya?" asked Johnny,

I certainly couldn't argue with his logic. Albeit only a brief respite before I set off to do this deed, Johnny and I were gypsies in the palace for the next few hours. One thing I have to say for Vinnie, he sure know how to live. We raided his little fridge, kicked back on the kitty queen and flipped on an episode of Animal Police' where they were arresting some scum who were running a cockfighting ring. Teehee... I love that show. Whatever jealousy or resentment that I had perceived on Johnny's part seemed to have vanished, at least for the time being.

NOT JUST A WALK IN THE PARK

Turned out, I'm allergic to caviar.

Who knew? I nearly rubbed the fur right off my hide on every street lamp, telephone pole and tree between Park Avenue and the 64th Street entrance to the park.

During the winter months, the Central Park Carousel is only operated on weekends, and movie crews often prefer to shoot a movie at times when there will be fewer bystanders to get in the way of the cameras or hassle the actors. The darkness would also be beneficial to our operation as well.

By the time I arrived, the film crew were already setting up their equipment, and the actors portraying a pair of lovers were rehearsing their lines in one of the carriages which offered rides through the park. The paved road where the carriages drive is a good distance from the carousel house, which sat down in a little gully, so we would be relatively shielded from onlookers. The film crew would likely pay no attention to a couple of cats, as long as we didn't interfere with the lighting or get into the camera shots.

I looked around for Mr. Smith's associate, who had been described to me as a Tortoise cat with an incredibly bad haircut. I suppose because of his breed and the tendency of organizations such as ours to give everyone nicknames, he was called "The Turtle". Since Mr. Turtle was nowhere in sight (and I sincerely hoped he would be a no-show), I decided to have a closer look at the carousel. I'd never had an opportunity to tour the park since moving here from Philly. It was a beautiful ride with over fifty hand-carved wooden horses. The carousel was brought over to Central Park from Coney Island after the original was lost in a fire. I could just imagine the sound of the calliope music and children laughing as they rode the colorful horses round and round. Mothers would stand on the platform and hold their little one's cotton candy and frozen lemonade. It was beautiful.

I was briskly shaken from my daydream of ponies and sugarplums as Turtle knocked me from the carousel's platform into the operator's pit. I saw stars when my head hit one of the brass mirrors on my way down. I came up swinging, but my first punch was stopped by Turtle's muscular foreleg.

"If you're done wit yer little merry-go-round ride, can we take care of bidness and git outta here before the mounted po-leece come riding through? Those are ponies with attitude – not old and tired like the carriage horses. I think the cops train 'em to stick up for 'em or sumthin. They'll kick the crap outta you if you even act like you're gonna run or get all up in the cop's face."

With that bit of information, Turtle produced a bag which contained two brightly colored glass stones. They were exactly the color and shape of two stones in the headpiece of the bedazzled Arabian carousel horse. Turtle and I had been chosen for this dubious task because we could likely complete our part of the operation undetected while the film crew was busy setting up their equipment, Even if we were spotted clawing at the carousel horse's jewelled headpiece, we'd just be shooed away as nuisances. Who would ever suspect two cats as

being involved in a jewel heist?

The job itself was a piece of cake. Earlier that week, a renowned jewel thief and his accomplice had stolen two of the largest loose diamonds in the world from a century-old jewelry design house on Fifth Avenue. After they made their getaway, the less recognizable accomplice had gone undetected to the carousel house in Central Park and replaced two of the glass simulated diamonds in the headpiece of the Arabian carousel horse with the priceless diamonds. There they would remain until the heat was off, and then they would be retrieved and taken overseas and sold on the black market.

Today, it was our job to claw the diamonds out of the headpiece and leave the original fake stones on the ground beneath the horse, That way, when it was discovered that the stones were missing, they would easily be found lying within plain sight right on the platform under the horse.

The thought crossed my mind that this really wasn't a job which should require two of us to complete. But as I finished removing the diamonds and turned around to get the fake stones from Turtle, I saw his tail swishing in the air as he batted the two stones back and forth between his front paws like marbles. Ah, now it was clear why I'd been called in to ensure the job was done properly. A lot of bosses hire associates who aren't the sharpest knives in the drawer, simply because they're too stupid to figure out the workings of the organization; thus they aren't likely to rat anyone out if they get caught. Also, if it goes down wrong, they're expendable.

I made sure that Turtle watched every move I made, so that he could report back to Mr. Smith that I had completed my part of the mission successfully. The final portion of the job was a little trickier. With teamwork, we managed to get the real diamonds back into the drawstring pouch. Turtle at least was helpful in pulling the strings on the pouch to close it securely. Now we were to nonchalantly go out into the crowd that was gathering to watch the movie being shot. The sweethearts who had been casually out for a carousel ride would ask the driver to let them out to watch the filming. They would then sit down on the park bench nearest the entrance to the Carousel House. The girl would *ooh* and *ah* over the sweet little kittens, one of which had the tiny velvet pouch in his mouth. She would pocket the pouch and our job would be complete.

All went exactly as planned. The fake stones

were lying on the platform beneath the Arabian horse and I had successfully carried the little pouch containing the real diamonds in my mouth to the waiting couple. As she gave me belly rubs, the lady had taken the pouch from me and slipped it into her coat pocket.

Turtle disappeared as quickly has he had arrived. I decided that there was no reason to waste an opportunity to see Central Park, so I gave myself a little tour. I recognized many places that I'd seen while sitting with the family as they watched TV shows and movies. I saw the frozen lake where skaters were gliding across the ice. The entire park was magical. Twinkling white lights decorated the tree-lined cobblestone paths. The mounted policemen rode through the park on horses groomed to perfection.

As I circled back around to the carousel, I saw that the actors and actresses had arrived, as well as dozens of extras. As if by magic, it was no longer winter in that section of the park. Everyone was wearing summer clothing from another era. There were men in red and white striped shirts with white Panama hats and ladies in long skirts with bustles and parasols. The carousel had been brought to life with glistening colored lights and wonderful music coming from the calliope.

The jewel thieves were now standing behind the rope which separated the movie scene from the crowd of observers. Although they were mere observers, they too were playing a role. I thought they were quite convincing in their roles as young lovers. Apparently, New York's finest didn't agree. As the mounted police sat tall in their saddles monitoring the crowd and ensuring the safety of the film crew and actors, one of them began to scroll on his handheld computer. He and his partner spoke for a second, and then rode their horses in opposite directions, dismounted and began to walk into the crowd. With one officer on either side of the couple, they very efficiently and quietly handcuffed both of the obviously-identified suspects and walked them down the cobblestone path to a waiting police car.

Somehow, I had managed to complete my assignment and at the same, justice had been done. It was the perfect ending to a long, but extremely interesting day.

I headed back across the river to the safety and security of my home. I had never been so grateful for leftovers. Never before had my bed felt so warm and cozy. Vinnie wasn't expected back into the city until the following day, so I got a solid twelve hours... and so did my conscience.

THAT'S MY STORY AND I'M STICKING TO IT

My family was sitting at the dinner table when I finally woke. I sauntered into the kitchen, stretching and yawning with every other step. Lucy ran to hug me, but she was told to wash her hands and get busy eating her broccoli. I had no idea what broccoli is, but I would've given it a try. I was starving. The mother excused herself from the table and went to the laundry room to pour a bowl of dry cat food for me. Well, it was a start I guess. The woman is a saint. Truly she is. She carried the bowl of dry, nondescript food back into the kitchen and poured a ladle of sauce from her chicken cacciatore over the little pellets. How did she know I'm Italian? I mean I assume that I am Italian. I was born in the Italian Marketplace in Philly and I was born behind the Italian deli. Cook was Italian. Yeah, I'm definitely Italian.

I hadn't heard anything from Vinnie, so I hoped that if he *had* returned as scheduled from the Hamptons, he was all tucked into his big ole kitty king, sleeping off his overindulgence of rich food. Tonight, I would've been content to curl up in front of the fireplace with the family while they're watching TV, but that was not to be. Fifteen minutes into a rerun of Princess Diaries, I heard scratching on the laundry room screen. That was usually the signal that one of the boys had arrived with a message from Vinnie. I got up and went into my room and sure enough, there was Johnny, sharpening his claws like he was going into battle with a sabre-toothed tiger.

I slipped out through the pet door and asked Johnny what message he had for me. I prayed it wasn't a job for tonight. I didn't have the strength for anything physical, not even a walk uptown. Johnny was fidgeting and wringing his hands as he walked in circles. His clothes were soaked in sweat, despite the fact that it was only 31 degrees. I asked what was going on, but I thought I might already know the answer.

"I knew trouble was brewing as soon as the Missus' SLS AMG Mercedes pulled into the parking garage and I saw Vinnie pacing in the back window and leaving claw marks in the Italian leather upholstery," Johnny began.

"What was wrong? Me and Turtle carried out our part of the mission without a hitch." I quickly interjected, "Not our fault the accomplices got arrested."

"I have no clue. There was no talking to Vinnie. When he got inside the condo, he climbed up on the top of the cherry bookcase unit in the library and turned the whole thing over. Some of those books were rare first editions! The Missus went bananas," said Johnny. By this time, my mouth was agape and I kinda felt bad that Johnny had witnessed this breakdown,

Johnny continued, becoming more and more animated with every recollection. "Then Vinnie went into the pantry and started knocking all the cans off the shelves and their Greek cook was jumping up and down and screaming something I didn't understand and pointing to the dents in the cans. Next thing I knew, the Missus did something no one, (including Vinnie) ever thought she'd do – she had the butler throw Vinnie outside!"

I was in utter shock. The Great Vincent Van Gato, tossed out on his one, pathetic ear like common trash! Oh tell me more.

The butler apparently was more than happy to comply. He's been putting up with Vinnie coming in at all hours and leaving a trail of garbage behind him for years. When he leaves the suite it looks like a tornado has ripped through it. The maids all complain to the butler and threaten to quit and he'll eventually have to talk to the Missus about it. That never goes well, because, until today, she thought Vinnie could do no wrong and it just makes the staff look like a bunch of whiners. So anyway, I slipped outside as the butler came back in from 'taking out the trash', so to speak, and there was Vinnie, lying in a snow drift with only his back legs sticking out. I was afraid to go near him, but when I saw him struggling to get out of the snow bank, I figured I'd better help or I'd catch it for just standing there. You've gotta come, Frankie. It's bad, It's real bad."

Once again, I didn't know whether to believe

a thing that Johnny was saying, but he was shaking so bad when he was recounting it all that I tended to believe him. Apparently, the shock of the Missus' reaction to his reign of terror or the ice and snow or a combination of both had cooled Vinnie's temper. Johnny said he was pretty calm when he sent for me. The only message was, "Tell Frankie we need to talk. He'll know why." And so I did.

What I wouldn't know until much later was that Johnny wasn't the dupe I believed him to be. After all, before I came along, he had been in the number two position in the organization.

Granted, Vinnie wasn't exactly Einstein. His only education was from the School of Hard Knocks, so the bar wasn't set all that high. But that night, Johnny played me as sweetly as a violin in the New York Philharmonic.

I'd been expecting to hear from Vinnie as soon as Mr. Smith contacted him, which I assumed was shortly after the six o'clock news hit the air and word reached the Hamptons that the accomplices of the jewel thief had been caught. While the ladies in the social circle in which the Missus ran might not be aware of unrest in the Middle East, news of two hunks of diamond being stolen from a store on Fifth Avenue to which they paid weekly – and sometimes daily – homage was sure to have gotten their attention. Oddly enough, I had been uncharacteristically calm as I waited for it all to go down. Despite Johnny's rendition of Vinnie's tirade, I was calm as a cucumber, because my part in the events had been played to perfection. Turtle could vouch for that and I, in return, would vouch for the fact that Turtle was superb in his role as useless bystander.

Even though I remained composed, as I made

my way up to Manhattan to meet with Vinnie, I did begin to put together a scenario that I would play out with him. I decided to lead with the truth. I had done exactly what Mr. Smith asked of me. I met Turtle. I removed the diamonds from the horse's headpiece. I made sure the colored glass replicas were in plain sight beneath the horse, and I gave the lady the bag with the real diamonds. The proof was in the pudding (or velvet pouch in this case). The cops had found the jewels on her when they handcuffed and frisked her. I had left when Turtle did and I took a little tour of the park on my way out. When I came full-circle, I saw the cops making the bust. If it got right down to it, those two cops could probably identify me because one of their horses nearly stepped on me as I was trying to maneuver in to get a better view of the arrest. OK, we'd leave that part out. It's never good to have someone who can identify you.

Vinnie had me thoroughly checked out before he brought me into his organization. He'd even remarked a time or two that my reputation was the most pristine of his boys. Every one of the others had some kind of mark on their record.

They'd been arrested before.

When we arrived at the condo, Vinnie was shivering in the vestibule between the revolving door and the entrance to the lobby. The doorman had taken pity on him and let him sit under the big hot air blower to take the chill off and dry out from his eviction into the snow bank. The doorman had never liked Vinnie any more than the butler, housekeeper, cook and staff who had to deal with him on a daily basis. He was brash, impertinent, rude, discourteous and, oh yes – spoiled. But right now, he was wet and cold and almost humble.

Vinnie refused to look at us when Johnny and I entered the lobby. The fact that the doorman even let us into the building was a surprise. He didn't even hesitate when he saw us peering in at Vinnie through the front glass; he opened the emergency door and stood blocking us from view of passersby and incoming residents as we slipped inside. We hid behind a potted palm in the lobby until the residents went on upstairs and then he motioned for us to get into the elevator. He even unlocked the code to send the elevator on up to the penthouse for us and said to take our little buddy up and see if we could sweet-talk his way back in. I'd only been in the penthouse the one time before while Vinnie was in the Hamptons and I had climbed up the downspout that time. When the elevator doors opened, I expected a hallway like in a hotel, but it opened right into the living room. Vinnie was shaking bad now. Maybe from being wet and cold, but I think at least part of it was nerves. The butler started walking towards us, rolling up his sleeves, as if he was preparing to grab us all by the scruff of the neck and throw us down the elevator shaft; but before he reached where we were standing, Vinnie let out a cry worse than any female cat I've ever heard caterwauling. Had he been a little kitten, that cry would've caused the mother cat to start lactating. As it was, the Missus who had been ensconced in a tufted, leather sofa in front of a stone fireplace, stood up holding a glass containing a couple of fancy ice cubes and a couple of fingers of a golden brown liquid. She kind of smirked at the sight of Vinnie standing there quaking with his head all tilted to the side and his bottom lip in a pout.

She walked over to him and said, "Now

little man, what's momma going to do with you? What on Earth possessed you to destroy our lovely home like that? Don't you appreciate all I've provided for you?" With that, Vinnie went in for the kill. He began wrapping himself around her legs and purring. It was enough to

make you want to throw up. But apparently, it was a tried and true tactic that worked, and she heaved a sigh of defeat and carried Vinnie over by the massive fireplace to warm up.

"Lucinda, please fetch some of the Porthault bath sheets – one for Vinnie and one for each of his guests," the Missus said to the housekeeper, who scurried off to obey the Missus' order.

Before I knew what hit me, I was wrapped in the softest, thickest, Egyptian cotton bath sheet and laid in front of the largest fireplace I'd ever seen in my entire life. The logs were the size of whole trees. Why, a man six foot tall could stand up straight inside the fireplace.

As if that weren't a grand enough gesture, the Missus pulled on a tapestry cord and immediately, the chef appeared.

"Our boys here must be starved to death, poor darlings," she commented to the chef, who appeared more than a little disgusted that he was being asked to cater to even more animals. "They need bowls of warm milk for each of them and a platter of filet mignon sliced across the grain in bite sized pieces, please." I caught just a glimpse of Vinnie wearing a big Cheshire cat grin, for just a second, before he switched his mask from comedy to tragedy once again for effect when she turned back to him.

"There now, darlings – you'll feel much better as soon as you warm up and get those little tummies full" With that, the Missus gave each of a pat on the head and a gentle belly rub. It felt really nice, but her Chanel #5 nearly bowled me over.

After we finished dining on the thinly sliced, broiled to perfection, rare steak, I lapped up all of the warm milk from a Staffordshire bone china bowl. Between the full belly, a soft towel, warm fire and warm milk, I could barely hold my eyes open. I began to yawn, and just before I fell hopelessly into a deep sleep, I noticed that Vinnie was now curled up in the Missus' lap and was giving her his best repentant licks on the hand. I looked around for Johnny and saw his empty towel and realized that he was no longer with us. I dreamt of palaces with servants at my beck and call, and silver trays of meat which took four men to carry to my table. When I next awoke, I was back in the real world, outside in a frozen holly bush with Vinnie nudging me with his greasy nose. The Vinnie we all knew and feared was back and the inquisition regarding my failed assignment was about to begin.

I'm not going to tell you it went flawlessly, because Vinnie trusts *no one*. He must've asked me the same questions six times each.

"Kid, where were the hitches in the plan?"

"None from our perspective, Vinnie. We did everything just as we were told."

"Is there anything that Smith could trace back to you that might've tipped off the cops and caused them to pick up the guy and girl?"

"No. Nothing I can think of."

"When you carried the pouch to the woman, was it stickin' out yer mouth so's somebody coulda seen?"

"I don't think so, Vinnie. Matter of fact, I was so careful to conceal it that I nearly choked on the darn thing. Oh maybe the little string might've hung out, but I'm pretty sure if it did, it probably looked like a mouse's tail or something. People around her were all smiling at me and one lady said I was cute."

"Well ain't that loverly?" Vinnie cuffed me once across the jowls. "Get serious, boy. This is bidness."

"Ow! Alright, Vinnie," I said, rubbing the sting away. "What about the Turtle? Did he pull any boneheaded screw ups?"

"No, Vinnie. Like I said, it all went exactly as planned. I saw one of the cops on a little handheld computer. Maybe somebody sent him a picture of the couple or something. You said yourself; it's been all over TV."

"Yeah, I guess you're right," admitted Vinnie. "Everybody's always looking for somebody else to blame. It happens. Deals go wrong. Ok, we'll let it go now. Good job, Kid."

When he'd finally stopped grilling me, (and the only reason he stopped then was because he was hungry and it was cold as a well digger's knee outside), and have given me the usual atta-boy, a pat on the back he muttered to himself a bit and then returned to the comforts of his condo and the woman who loved him.

Unbeknownst to me, Vinnie went over to the park after our talk that day, just to see the carousel. I suppose he wanted to get a feel for where everything happened. I guess there must've been a sign or something near the building that housed the carousel that told of its history. Grasping at tidbits of history always made him hold his head a little higher and his chest protrude just a tad over his enormous belly. Vinnie had read that a Brooklyn firm called Stein & Goldstein crafted the carousel back in 1908, so from that day forward, the caper was to be known as the Stein & Goldstein incident (S&G for short).

Fortunately for me and for Vinnie, Mr. Smith placed all the blame for the bust on the couple with whom I'd placed the diamonds. He said they were just amateurs who never should've been hired by the primary perpetrator. They were consider disposable. No effort was made to provide them with representation at their trial. The diamonds would be held in evidence until the case was closed, at which time they would be returned to the store from which they were stolen. As for the mastermind behind the robbery, well I heard that he was on an extended vacation in Brazil.

I returned to the comfort of my modest home. It wasn't the penthouse, but there was more genuine love there than in a mansion on Park Avenue. There wasn't filet mignon in our house, but Mom could really cook! She was part Irish and part Italian, so no matter what leftovers I got, they were going to give me gas, but it was so worth it. Being the only two testosterone units in the household, Dad and I had little contests after supper to see who could run the girls out of the family room first. It was a time when, despite the old man's allergies, we really bonded.

Did you see what I did there? I'm calling them Mom and Dad now. I'm glad Vinnie told me to lay low until the whole incident blew over. I need time to examine my career decision. I'm feeling a definite shift in my priorities. Take my perception of Vinnie for example. When we first met, it shook me to my very foundation when he spoke. I've shared with you how I feared Vinnie in the beginning. That's not to say that I think him any less dangerous now, but I see him more for what he truly is – a user and a charlatan. Vinnie likes to imagine himself as the Feline Godfather who runs the whole of New York State and everyone in it. As if his vocabulary doesn't betray him, he pretends that he is well educated. Obviously, charisma goes a long way because there are hundreds, if not thousands, of street cats in this country who believe every word of the bill of goods that Vinnie has been selling for the last ten years. He may not have been blessed with a superior intellect, but Vinnie has a PhD in street smarts.

Then there's that matter of his inability to trust anyone. I've learned that comes from the insecurity created by a rocky start in life, much like my own. But on hearing Vinnie's story, I realized that I was actually quite lucky. Maybe because I was with Goo who was blind, animals like Luther and old Gustopher befriended us and showed us the ropes. Vinnie grew up in Harlem. His mother died of starvation just a couple of weeks after he was born, leaving eleven kittens inside a wrecked car in the salvage yard to fend for themselves. There were so many junk cars piled up on top of each other that nobody even knew they were there. His mother had scavenged the few scraps of food she could find on the floorboards of the cars, and sometimes if the trunk or glove box had popped open from the impact of the collision, she would score some real snacks. But the food was always stale and never healthy. With eleven babies to nurse, her little body just couldn't find enough nutrition to keep her going. The kitten's eyes had just been open a few days when their mother died. Strictly on instinct did they leave their mother's lifeless body and venture out of the car in search of their next meal. It was only by chance that the crane operator saw the kittens as they tumbled out of the broken windshield onto the hood of the car. He had been about to lift the car onto a stack to be crushed into scrap metal when he saw something roll across the hood. At first, he thought it was rats running from the noise of the machinery. But there were so many of them and in such a rainbow of colors he knew they couldn't be rats, so he shut off the engine and climbed down to have a look. In another week or two, the kittens would have been so feral that he might not have been able to catch them all, but given their wobbly little legs and lack of strength due to hunger, he was able to round them all up into a cardboard box, which he sat out by the gate at lunchtime with a sign that said, 'FREE KITTENS – HELP YOURSELF'. By quitting time that day, the box was empty. Hard to say what became of them, but in that poor neighborhood, their chances of survival were slim. The tales Vinnie told of his youth were bone chilling.

The methods he was called upon to ensure his survival were appalling. Little wonder that he has not an ounce of compassion or trust for neither man nor animal.

EASTSIDE/WESTSIDE - ALL AROUND THE TOWN

By the time summer finally rolled around, I had participated in every job imaginable. Vinnie knew that I wasn't going to pull anymore jobs that were the scope of the S&G Caper, so he threw a few jobs Johnny's way and I had a few day's breather, but regardless of whether I was on assignment from Vinnie or whether I was just minding my own business, trouble seemed to always find me.

I ♥ NY, and I am no longer a tourist. I know all five boroughs like the back of my paw and I've developed a bit of a reputation, so NY knows me. People in my neighborhood walk to the other side of the street when they see me coming. Some of the neighbors have even called

Mom and Dad to complain that I'm a nuisance and troublemaker, but all the family sees is their sweet, adorable little pussycat. They think all the neighbors are just jealous. Ha!

There's an old guy three doors down who lives alone. Never been married, and he has an English flower garden in his backyard with an eight foot high brick wall around it. He grows what I'm told are very rare flowers and shows them in the city every spring at the Annual Garden Show. I've gone past his house at all hours of the night and seen him in his basement with special lights on the seedlings and he was talking to them. I've even heard him playing classical music to the flowers. I'm not going to criticize though. To each his own. He must be onto something because he always wins blue ribbons. I doubt that he would be so generous with his assessment of me.

About one am, I was coming home from a well-deserved night on the town when I saw this absolutely drop-dead gorgeous Siamese female of the feline variety walking on top of the old gardener's brick wall. Now, you know that my status was abruptly changed from tomcat

to eunuch over a year ago, right? So I don't howl and prowl as it were. But I have 20/20 vision and I appreciate a beautiful girl when I see one. Well, she apparently found me to be irresistibly handsome. She kept making the little kissy pout with her lips and swishing her lovely tail and those eyes – oh those ice-blue, almond shaped eyes! I was mesmerized by those eyes. She must've felt the same way about my eyes, because our gazes locked on one another and then *wham*! She walked right into a tree limb that spilled over the garden wall. I watched helplessly as she lost her footing and fell over into the garden. She began to howl because it seemed she had fallen into the middle of one of the gardener's Rugosa rose bushes. He had purposely selected the Rugosa hybrid hedges to plant around the circumference of the wall to discourage intruders. While the silvery pink flowers are fragrant and incredibly lovely and the hedge extremely hardy and resistant to the frigid northern winters, they have inch-long, wicked thorns which were piercing the flesh of my beautiful Asian she-cat.

I immediately sprung into action. I swiftly scaled the wall, lightly pouncing across the thorny hedges, and landing on the invisible laser beam that tripped the security alarm. All manner of bells, buzzers and whistles fragmented the silence. Somewhere at Con Ed, a meter was spinning wildly as thousands of watts of lights illuminated the entire block. I managed to grab the front leg of the damsel in distress and freed her from her ghastly knife-like prison; however, in doing so, I managed to tear her fragile, silky coat and catch her delicate lavender collar on the sprinkler head of the irrigation system, thus turning on the water and showering us both. The entire chain reaction lasted less than two minutes, which was the precise amount of time that it took the gardener to jump from his bed, slide his feet into his slippers, throw on his bathrobe and grab his cell phone, so that he could dial the police on his way down the staircase.

I, of course, was beyond the garden wall as soon as I could extricate myself from the situation. I had allowed a pretty face to deter me from my appointed rounds, and it will probably happen again. I *hope* it happens again, for such is the spice of life.

🐾 🐾 🐾

I soon grew weary of having too much time on my hands and I let the boss know that I was ready to get back to work. I found out later that while I'd been away, Johnny had done everything in his power to usurp his position as the boss' confidante and sidekick. His plot seemed to be working, because the first assignment I had upon my return was just a bit of fluff. But when I heard the details, I didn't put up a fuss. It would allow me to revisit my childhood. I had been a child only in chronological age. I had never experienced the joy of carefree play, because Goo and I were always struggling for survival.

Although we were just kittens, we couldn't frolic in the sunshine because we were always looking over at shoulders for the dangers which lurked on the streets.

The circus was in town – well actually outside of town—for three glorious weeks. Vinnie had a little protection racket going with some of the local small business owners. The deal was the shop owners gave us sellable merchandise in exchange for Vinnie having a couple of the boys keep an eye on their shop during peak burglary hours. We were usually around during those hours anyway, so it was like taking candy from babies. If we happened to *be* the burglars as well, then it was win/win. We didn't have to lift the merchandise, because they were handing it to us for free!

A circus has, shall we say, unique security concerns. Local law enforcement has never been particularly enthusiastic about addressing those concerns, so Vinnie figured maybe we could do a little bartering. Now, I don't know if the S&G Caper had been a little more than Vinnie had bargained for as well, or if he was tired, or if he was just having one of his rare moments when he

wanted to do something good, but what he had planned for the circus job benefitted a good many animals. Without sounding condescending, I was actually proud of Vinnie and eager to take part in this job when he explained it to me.

"Here's how I see this goin' down, kid. I want ya to go to the fairgrounds and wait for the circus to arrive. Get all chummy with the animal performers. You make 'em all believe that you can run interference between the circus, the townspeople, and the law during their stay, see. Then, when they get loaded up to leave town, you get yer new pals – the biggest and strongest of 'em – to help you rig their feed trailer so that, as they drive out of town, all of the torn hundred pound bags of food would real slow like, fall out of the holes that you punch in the floor of the trailer, and they leave a trail of food for all the other animals in New Jersey and maybe even on into New York who ain't got homes and food and all. If you do it just right, the circus will be long gone, the food all eaten and nobody will be the wiser." It amazed me that Vinnie had thought this all through so thoroughly.

When the tractor trailers full of everything

from jumbo tents to Jumbo the elephant arrived, I was there to introduce myself to the four-legged performers and outline my list of services. When the animal caravans arrived, it was like the landing of Noah's Ark. There were at least two of almost every animal and more of some – there were two lead horses (Prince and Sheherazade); the lions (Timba and Sikare), chimpanzees (Champ and Nanette), the bears (Theodore and Ursula), the white tiger (Beatrice) and Otis, the Bengal, a donkey (Yoohoo) and my favorites –

the elephants (Annabelle and Benny).

Everyone was eager to help, and of course, there were the inevitable questions, but even as the questions were posed, the rest of the group came up with solutions.

"So you mean that some of us will actually tear holes in the floor of the trailer? If the trainers find out we did it, I hate to think of the consequences," said Timba.

"There's not one of us here that doesn't know how to lock and unlock our cages. They never know when we've been out. They'll see us all back where we should be and never imagine that we're responsible in any way," reassured Ursula.

And then Benny asked the question I had been anticipating:

"If we're going to spill most of the food out of the trailer, what are we going to eat when it's all gone?" Otis, the oldest and largest of the Bengal tigers, quickly allayed their worries. "I've been travelling on this circuit for many years and they always stopover in Burlington to restock the feed supply. When the cage boys and trainers go to count feed bags and load their new order, they will see what has been spilled and have to replenish the stock. Now is everybody on board to help Frank here feed our friends in Jersey?" With nods of heads, Operation Feed the Homeless (OFTH) was unanimously approved. But first, it was time to build us a circus! .

It was really hard to contain my excitement as I watched the stakes being driven into the ground and the big tents going up. I sat perched on the top of the ticket booth as I watched the magic that is the circus unfold.

Soon the performers began to arrive. They carried trunks laden with sequined costumes. There were even costumes for some of the animals. As the performers continued to help unload the trailers, a bus carrying some very strange looking individuals arrived. I later learned that these people were actually what were called the side-show attractions. I'm told that some humans pay money to point fingers and ridicule other humans who have some disfigurement or unusual characteristic. That just doesn't seem right to me. I would take offense if someone were to put me on display so that other cats could come and poke fun at my scars.

Once the tents were up, the lights in place and the trapezes and tightropes strung, the performers, (both human and animal), began rehearsals. I watched in absolute awe and amazement. Even with our superior balance and agility, cats would never dare to attempt the skilled feats of the trapeze artists and acrobats. I've got to tell you, since my 'accident', I get a little vertigo if called upon to scale to any significant heights.

On the night of dress rehearsal, there was a tiny little woman, ironically named Ariel, in a pink tutu walking two stories in the air across a one inch wide rope that stretched nearly twenty-five feet across the width of the Big Top. Her hair was twisted up into a bun and secured with a little diamond tiara. It shone like spun gold beneath the twinkling lights. On her feet were pink satin ballet slippers and she carried nothing more than a parasol to help her maintain balance as she walked along the tightrope. Ariel was the most beautiful lady I have ever seen to this day. I'm not ashamed to tell you that, were she a cat, I would have pledged my heart to her right then and there. You can imagine my amazement when a man climbed up that ladder carrying a unicycle and proceeded to ride it across that same tightrope! I don't know what the pay is for circus performers, but whatever it is, it's not enough.

Later in the show there was an act they called liberty riding, where a dozen or so horses galloped around the ring with no reins or tack, other than some sequined headpieces. They were trained to verbal and visual commands used by the trainer. Well, out comes Ariel again. This time she was standing on the back of Prince as he galloped into the ring. Mid-way around the ring, she even jumped from Prince's back to Sheherazade's and then stood on her head as they cantered! Maybe she did have a bit of cat in her after all. Her balance and skill were unequalled in any human.

I loved watching the jugglers practice tossing fire batons back and forth and the contortionists bending themselves like pretzels. One thing I *didn't* like about the circus was the clowns. Now I know that clowns are supposed to make you laugh. They're silly and funny and ride in cars that are far too small and honk horns that make annoying sounds and wear ridiculously large red shoes. But I simply don't trust anyone who spends the biggest portion of their day hiding behind a face covered in white grease paint with painted on eyes, painted on lips, an orange fright wig, and a rubber nose. There just seems something sinister about disguising oneself in that manner. One place you would never catch me is backstage in what they called Clown Alley. It was where they kept all their clown equipment and put on their peculiar clown makeup.

The offer I made to the animals to provide protection in return for their help with OFTH during their stay had been met with muffled laughs. When I thought about it later, I guess even a seemingly worldly tough guy like myself would not be seen as a deterrent to anyone when standing alongside lions and tigers and bears. Oh my, come on Vinnie. Once again, I had egg on my face. But circus is good people. They kindly thanked me for my offer and invited me to stay with them until they pulled up stakes, which of course was an offer I would never have refused, but it would mean being away from home for three days.

I had stayed out a night or two before a couple of times when Vinnie had a job that demanded it. The first time, the family freaked out because they imagined that I'd been hit by a car or catnapped or something. When I'd finally returned home, they lavished all manner of food and toys on me. It made me feel kind of bad that I'd caused them such worry and heartache. But then Lucy took to carrying me all over the house like a rag doll and it was time for me to hit the road again. I decided that the best way to keep them from being concerned was to stay overnight someplace every now and then, just so they'd get used to it and not worry. I'd be gone several nights this time, but they wouldn't worry much now that I had them trained.

On opening night, the colored lights which adorned the circus tents mingled with the myriad of headlights on the stream of cars lined up all the way to Hoboken. Thousands came to walk the midway, eat the peanuts and cotton candy, and play the games, then top off the evening with the main show under the Big Top. After watching the setup and hours of rehearsal, it was magical to see it all come together with the roar of the crowd and the thunderous applause. By that time, I wanted nothing more than to be a ringmaster in a red, double-breasted jacket with shiny gold buttons and braid, white breeches, black boots, a top hat and a whip. I even volunteered to work without pay. Everyone chuckled a little.

After all of the human performers had long-since turned in for the night, I was privileged to see a side of the circus that even they had never seen. I was just about to find myself a place to sleep for the night when Theo, Prince, Timba and Benny came looking for me.

"What's up guys?" I asked, and then suddenly realized that the four were roaming the fairgrounds free. "Wait a minute, I just saw your trainers put you in your cages before they headed off to bed. How'd you get out?" My questions were still hanging in the air when around the corner came some of the girls: Annabelle, Beatrice, Sikare and Ursula. Nanette had hitched a ride on Annabelle's back. "We wish you could come along with us, Frank. Maybe we could teach you some tricks to show the trainers and they'd bring you with us," said

Nanette, the Chimp.

"Yeah, we trained two chimps to pick locks for those of us without opposable thumbs!" Yoohoo, the donkey chided, as he and Prince joined the party.

We were all becoming fast friends. They all liked me and they trusted me with the biggest secret known only to circus animals.

"Should we let Frankie in our little secret boys and girls?" Benny asked just as Otis made his appearance, scratching himself and rubbing the sleep from his eyes.

"Kids, if you don't stop partying all night, you're gonna look as old and tired as me. You'll be shipped off to the dog food factory and there'll be no more stardom for none of ya. Awww, come on. Lighten up. I was just pulling yer legs. Come on over here Frank, and I'll educate you a little more about our life in the circus. You see, people are always talking about being afraid to go to the circus because they're afraid one of the big cats might get loose and eat someone or an elephant might go on a rampage or something. Before allowing a circus to come into their town, the authorities always make a big deal about security measures and they assure everyone that all these wild, vicious animals will be held in secure cages. Well I'm going to give away one of our little trade secrets. You see, if Timba or, say, Teddy here, were truly hungering for humans, no cage is going to contain them. We're all placed under lock and key by the trainers every night, and as soon as all of the humans are snug in their beds and fast asleep, we all have a really good time. The next morning, when the handlers came around to feed, everyone is where they should be and all locks are secure. I'll say no more, except to say, we're a team and we have the, errrrr... equipment necessary to come and go as we please. We just know which side our bread's buttered on, so we choose to stay."

Before any of us were ready to say goodbye, it was closing night. After the last of the patrons left the fairground, everyone went to work immediately tearing down tents and pulling up stakes so that they could leave town at dawn the following morning. Finally, around midnight, the last trailer was loaded, the last stake removed from the fairgrounds, the last steamer trunk closed and all of the employees had been to the

Seventeen Wagon to pick up their pay checks, and then gone to their beds for a few brief winks of sleep.

My new friends quietly made their way to the food trailer where I sat waiting to begin Operation Feed the Homeless. Each member of our team had been assigned their duties and they eagerly went to work.

Timba and Sikare used their razor-like claws to pepper the floor of the trailer with slits and holes.

"Come on Sikare, punch the holes big enough for the food to really flow!," said Timba.

"I think I just broke a claw!" replied Sikare, examining her sore paw. Timba rolled his eyes as does any male whose mate tells him she broke a nail to get out of work.

Annabelle and Benny, dragged the heavy bags of feed strategically over the holes. The trailer had already been hitched to the cab of the truck, so the next maneuver would be very tricky, but critical to the success of the operation. Prince and Sheherazade were to pull the front of the trailer up as Yoohoo pushed from the rear to angle it just enough that the food wouldn't begin to spill out until after it crossed the unavoidable trench which Champ and Nanette had been allowed to dig at the exit of the fairgrounds. Champ and Nanette were always getting into trouble, so when they were seen earlier sitting quietly digging with their little shovels and buckets, no one seemed to mind. At least they were staying out of the way for once.

The only step remaining was for Beatrice and Otis to very gently climb into the tenuously-positioned trailer and rip open all of the feed bags.

"Otis, I know your arthritis has been acting up, why don't you just go over there and sit down. I can handle this. It'll be fun to shred something for a good cause," Bea said, concerned for Otis' well-being.

"It's OK Bea. I want to do this. I want to be a part of giving back for all the years that I've been lucky enough to be fed and cared for by our handlers. I've heard the humans who come around from time to time and try to stir up trouble, saying that we're mistreated and that wild animals shouldn't be paraded on stage for money. But you know, we get medical attention whenever we need it. We're exercised daily to keep us in good shape and we get fed twice a day. We're never abused or treated badly. I mean, why would we be? If we were beaten, we'd be in poor physical condition and of no use to anyone. Yeah, there's definitely animals out there in a lot worse conditions than we are and we're going to give them at least one or two good meals. Now, come on Bea-let's get to work," Otis said as he motioned for Beatrice to get the bags nearest the door positioned and shredded.

Annabelle and Benny had just pushed the big steel doors of the trailer shut and secured themselves back into their enclosures when the drivers began to make their way to the Cook Shack for breakfast before hitting the road.

When the engines were all idling and ready to go, one of the big cats came looking for me. He said they had a little surprise for me back at the Tableau Wagon that held the rest of the show animals. Most circuses will use these ornamental show wagons to drive through town on their way to set up at the fairgrounds as a way to advertise. This troupe preferred to also *leave* town in style, so they would drive through town on full display as a final farewell to all who had patronized their show. Once through the town, they would pull off the road, lead the animals to water and then load them into the comfort of a trailer before hitting the interstate.

The trainer opened the door of the Tableau Wagon and allowed the big cat to take his place for the parade. As he did so, all the other animals turned in unison and looked wistfully at me. I guess pretty much everyone associated with the circus recognized that I'd be hanging around all week because I loved the circus. I'd passed muster as far as being an okay kind of guy, but what happened next was beyond my wildest expectations. The trainer lifted me up into the show wagon with the big cats and I rode into town as a star.

The last trailer to leave the fairgrounds was the one carrying the animal feed – the one that had been rigged to leak feed all over the roadways. As the Tableau Wagon in which we were riding hit the ditch dug by Champ and Nanette, it tilted a bit to the side and we ended up piled on top of each other in the corner. We didn't want to cause a scene or bring attention to the fact that this ditch might cause other trailers to be shuffled about, so we quickly all got to our feet and disbursed. Neither the truck behind us or the one pulling us seemed to pay any attention. There were always potholes and trenches wherever we went, so this one was of no concern.

When we pulled off the road on the other side of town to say our goodbyes, the driver of the feed truck remained in his vehicle. No traffic had been behind him on this isolated road, so if the feed was falling as we had planned, Operation Feed the Homeless was a complete success.

I turned to head back toward Brooklyn, when I heard the huge eighteen wheelers come to a screeching halt. I froze in my tracks but didn't turn around. I was afraid the damage to the truck, and the loss of costly food, had been discovered. I heard footsteps running towards me and the hair on my back stood at attention. The beautiful Ariel rubbed my head. "I'm sorry I never had time to tell you what a lovely, gentle cat you are. My stage name is Ariel. Isn't that a corny name for an aerialist? My real birth name is Barbara. I don't know where you came from, but I think that you stayed because you fell in love with the circus. It truly does get into your blood. I want you to have this to remember us by. She kissed the top of my head and placed a little heart charm onto my collar, on the ring that held my rabies tag. I never saw any of them again, but I would also never forget a single one of them, especially that wonderful lady.

As I strolled away from the convoy of circus trucks, I could see that we'd left a trail of food for as far as my eye could see. Animals of all species had already begun to pick at the food in the middle of the deserted roadway. When you're homeless, it doesn't matter if the food was intended for another species. If you're starving, you don't even care if it's tasty or if it's fresh, You take what you can get and you thank the good Lord for it. *Enjoy it guys*, I thought to myself. I felt so good that I'd been able to pay forward the good fortune I'd found with my family and I couldn't wait to get home.

I was exhausted and ready to go straight to bed, but I stopped to have a bite to eat and get a drink. ,I saw my reflection in my shiny aluminium water bowl and admired the little heart hanging around my neck. It looked to be real gold. Maybe it was Barbara before she became Ariel and wore cheap costume jewelry. Or maybe it had been her mother's who had died or left her when she was a little girl and she'd joined the circus to have a family. You just never know where people come from and how they got here. And then I saw that little heart was a locket. I shook it until it fell open. Inside the locket was a picture of a woman holding a little girl and on the other side was a tiny piece of golden hair. I knew the family would wonder how this locket got onto my collar, so I stuck a claw through the clasp and pulled until it finally gave way and dropped to the floor. I tucked carried it to my bed and pushed it into in a hole on the side where I had hidden my most precious possessions – the bone-shaped name tag from Luther's collar which had fallen off his collar one day when he broke free from his boy; a piece of a burlap bag that Goo and I slept on that first winter in the garage in Philly; and a tuft of black fur out of Snake's back. I kept that last memento to remind me that I still had a score to settle with Snake and someday, somehow I would.

"Thanks, Barbara," I whispered before falling blissfully asleep.

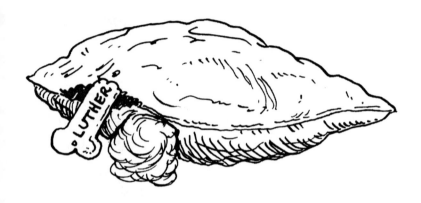

The next afternoon, I headed uptown to meet Vinnie and share the good news about the success of Operation Feed the Homeless. He was quite pleased with my report, but he didn't stick around to talk because it was the end of July and the midday heat was stifling.

I decided to treat myself to an air-conditioned train ride back across the river. Once again, I'd missed both breakfast and lunch and I had a craving for some good Chinese food. Best place I knew was over on Cook Street. It was the perfect time to do a little dumpster diving. I didn't have to dive for food now that I was a pet, but I liked to keep my skills honed and this was my neighborhood. I knew what was good and what was not. If you arrived after lunch and before the dinner crowd, you could always be assured of good, fresh food. Timing was everything during a heat wave.

Headfirst and wasting no time, I found a to-go box with hardly a spoonful of the delicious Moo Shoo Pork eaten. Obviously, someone's plans had changed suddenly. Their loss, my gain. I sat the box down under a shade tree to enjoy my meal, but just as I began to eat, I saw something across the street which forced me to become the second diner to have a change of plans.

A SIGHT FOR SORE EYES

It couldn't be. My mind had to be playing tricks on me. It's just wasn't possible. We were hundreds of miles from Philadelphia.

I crossed the street to have a closer look and in a crate which had just been removed from a car was my little brother. Goo was in New York! When I got to the parking space, the man carrying Goo's crate saw me looking through the wire door at him. Of course he had no idea who I was and Goo couldn't see me. But I could talk to him.

"Little brother, it's me, Frank. Is that really you, Goo?

Goo began to pace around in the crate and frantically bang against the door. The man carrying the crate had no idea who this other cat was or where he came from, but it seemed pretty clear the two wanted to investigate each other. So he set the crate carrying Goo down on the sidewalk and asked his wife to go on inside the photography studio and see if they were ready for Goo.

I moved closer to the crate and Goo relaxed, just knowing that not only was I still alive, but that I was well and living in NY. We knew that we didn't have much time, so I hurriedly began to fill Goo in the highlights of my life since the awful day when fate stepped in to separate us.

"Oh little brother, I didn't know what had happened to you. I didn't know if the Brawlers had hurt you or if you got away or... I was so scared for you," I began.

"Frank, is that really you? Oh Frank, I heard the people who came for you say that you were barely alive. I had no way of knowing if you made it or not. Are you OK Frank? Do you have any... are you... are you specially-abled now too, Frank?" Goo asked, afraid to hear the answer.

"Nah, I'm fine. Fat and healthy now. Oh that horrible Snake and his boys messed up my face a little, but I'm still handsome as ever," I said. "What about you Goo? You look amazing, You've put on some weight too, I see. And your so clean and, um... fluffy." I leaned in for a closer look and was pleased to see that Goo's tiny eyes no longer teared down his face as they had since his birth."Your eyes even look good, Goober. Are you still..."

"Blind? Yep. But the doctor says not totally. Remember I told you I could see fuzzy shadows and sometimes bright light? There's a big long name for it, but what it means is my eyes are just too little to see good like everybody else. It's called micro eyes or something. Well, Mom and Dad – oh wait, I forgot to tell you. I got adopted by these nice people. Scott and Colleen Angstadt. We live over in Jersey, and they're the most specialest people in the world. They gave me a whole room of my own, on accounta they've got six other cats and I just needed some time and space to myself, ya know. Anyhow, they buy me toys that I can sort of see and hear, so they're fun to play with. They take pictures of me all the time and, well one of the pictures won a contest or something and I'm here to get more pictures made for a magazine, Frank. I'm going to be on a magazine!"

"Aw man, that's great Goo," I said. "Sounds like you've got the best life any cat could ever ask for. You're finally getting to have the childhood you deserved. I'm so happy for you Goo."

I had friends over in Jersey, so I told him that it should be easy to find his house if I ever made it over that way .Goo seemed relieved to know that and said that he was glad to know that we might see each other again. I truly was relieved and happy that Goo was being so well cared for. I'm ashamed to admit that I'm a little jealous that he's getting to be a kid. But it's my own fault. I could be a house cat and play with toys and finish being a kid too; only I chose to be a thug and have to look over my shoulder every step of the way.

Thankfully, Colleen came out of the photographer's studio and motioned to Scott to bring Goo in before I had to figure out what to tell Goo about my life. Truth is, I was too ashamed.

"I'm adopted too," I shouted quickly. Then as Scott lifted Goo's crate, Goo shouted "Oh yeah and Frank, I met a great girl named Olivia and I have three sons back in Philly!"

"What? Well I—" but Goo was gone. What had I been about to tell him? 'Well I'm involved with the mob and I do horrible things that would make you ashamed of me?' I took the long way home. I had a lot of thinking to do about my life.

A LIFE UNEXAMINED

I'd had feelings of regret from time to time since I came to NY, but never had I been so ashamed as when I thought back on my conversation with Goo. Had we had more time together, what could I possibly have told him about my life since last we were together? Apparently, Goo had not only learned how to take care of himself, but had become a responsible cat with a family.

A cat is something of an enigma. On the one hand, me and Goo, we're two years old. We're considered 'adults' when we're a year old, but in a household setting, we like to play with toys until we're... well, old. Old is like maybe ten. So even though Goo was an adult tom out on the street with a family, once he got adopted, he's still a young cat who gets to play with toys. If he'd stayed on the streets, he might have had several dozen kittens by now. Thing is, then all those kittens and momma cats would've been homeless and scraping for food too. It was good that they fixed it so I didn't have a bunch of kittens. I wouldn't have been a good dad. I'm not much of a role model for anyone these days.

I know how lucky I am. I have everything I used to dream of back in Marconi Park. So why did I think I needed more excitement? Why did I have to have adventures and why oh why did those adventures involve a low-life like Vincent Van Gato and his brainless thugs?

Yes, I had a rough start in life like Vinnie, but I had enough leg-ups and good friends along the way to know right from wrong. My conscience is proof that I know right from wrong. A lot of cats go bad simply because of circumstances and because they fell in with the wrong crowd. Many never get a human family of their own and because of all the inbreeding, some of us just aren't bright enough to make it on our own. That wasn't the case with me. I'm smart. I have a brother who loves me. I had good people around me from the start. Cook, who owned the deli behind which me and Goo had been born, took the best care he could of me and Momma and Goo. He showed me what it was like to selflessly help someone in need – someone who had no possibility of ever being able to return the favor.

Then there was Luther, the Great Dane who befriended me and Goo after our mother was killed and we lived in Marconi Park. Luther was a gentle giant. He could easily have put Goo and I both out of misery with one swat of his humongous paw. But he brought us food and he befriended us, even though the other dogs in the neighborhood likely teased him for giving piggyback rides to two little kittens.

And good ole Gus. Gustopher was the old street cat who taught us more about survival. He had come into the old falling-down garage where me and Goo spent our first winter alone. The day Gus wandered in, he was just looking to grab himself a meal. Why would he spend time teaching me and Goo to hunt and eat mice? He had nothing to gain and mice to lose by doing so.

And now I have been adopted by a family who, although they are not financially well off, have furnished me with food, a bed of my own, a pet door so that I would be happy, and they truly love me. Mom loves it when I consent to sit in her lap and allow her to pet me and sometimes brush me. Lucy isn't as annoying as she used to be. I think she finally learned the difference between pets and toys. She's starting school this fall and I think I'm actually going to miss her. Then there's Dad. I really do enjoy sitting on the arm of his big leather recliner while he does guy things, like watching sports on TV and eating manly food. He always shares his summer sausage, cheese, pizza, hotdogs, or burgers with me.

So why can't all of this be enough? Why did I have to go looking for more? The day I met Vinnie, he told me that no one quits this job and he's said it countless times since then. But surely if I'm honest with him, he'll understand and let me out. He's got Johnny ready and willing to step back into my place as his #2 cat. What am I talking about? He would immediately think I had an ulterior motive. He'd probably think I'd signed on with someone else. He'd be all paranoid and figure I'm going to work for the competition. He'd never believe that anyone would want to leave him. He's just that conceited. But if I just explain that I want to go straight and not do anything unlawful or immoral again... no, that won't work. Vinnie definitely wouldn't understand conscience.

I decided to just take the coward's way out. I would just stay in my house. The family would assume that I got tired of roaming the streets and decided I have it pretty good with them after all. And that's true, except that I really do need fresh air and to see something besides the eight rooms and thirty-two walls of this house. And I've been seeing quite a lot of Giselle lately. She's the easiest-to-talk-to cat I've ever known and she understands me. She doesn't think badly of me for having sold my soul to the devil and signed on with Vinnie. I went over to talk to her the night after I saw Goo. I was pretty upset and confused and ashamed.

"Giselle," I'd said, "the best thing I could ever have wished for happened today. I found my little brother, Goo again. He's blind and yet he's made the most of the cards he's been dealt. Even though he's no longer with his kittens and their mother, he knows how lucky he is to have been adopted and found a good home. He appreciates everything he's given and it's enough. He's learned how to manage his blindness and it's not as if he's handicapped at all. He uses all his special abilities and he's more than able to do everything a sighted cat can do. So, Giselle, why can't I find my special abilities and use them for good?"

Giselle put her foreleg around my neck and kissed the top of my head. "Frank, you're one of the most special cats I know. You're smart. You're so much like my brother Nicky that sometimes it makes me sad, but then I think how lucky I am that you came into my life and that you are just like Nicky. It's like I have a little bit of him back, Nicky used to call it his wanderlust. He wanted to travel and see things and do new things. That's what I see in you, Frank. But you can do all those things without playing the dangerous games you're playing with Vinnie. I don't know what I'd do if someone else that I..."

She'd stopped and we didn't speak anymore about Vinnie that night, but I hoped that if she hadn't stopped talking, she would have said that she loves me. I think I love her too, But Giselle deserves better than me.

I spent the next three days inside. Vinnie sent Johnny to fetch me twice, but I didn't answer Johnny's scratches at the window. I stayed downstairs in the family room. Johnny wouldn't see me there because Dad kept the wooden blinds closed to cut down on glare on the wide screen TV. Of course, my food, litter box and bed were all in the laundry room and that was where Johnny always looked for me. Obviously, I couldn't ignore the call of nature or stop eating. I did find a new place to crash though. Lucy had wanted me to sleep in her bed from the beginning, but Mom didn't want cat hair in the bedrooms. I mean, that's something completely beyond my control and something every prospective cat owner should think about before they adopt. You can brush us till you're blue in the face, but we're going to shed. Sometimes worse than others, but it will happen. I just suggest you buy clothes and furniture the same color as your cat. Yeah that should work.

One night when Lucy was fast asleep, I nosed my way into her room and slipped up on the

foot of her bed. I knew that Mom or Dad always checked on her before they went to bed each night. If I could manage a really touching scene, they would have to let me stay with her. So very quietly, I slipped up on the pillow next to Lucy. I nuzzled her hair and gave her a couple of gentle kisses and then she put her arm across my neck. That was it. That was a Kodak moment. They would love it and I would have a new room. Sure enough, when Dad came in to tuck Lucy in, he looked down and saw us snuggled up together and went and fetched Mom to come see this precious scene. It worked! They left me there and when Lucy woke the next morning, she was thrilled to see her little kitty in bed with her,

Now to get my food and litter box moved. The following day, I refused to eat; that's something which former street cats never do. They never miss a meal. When Mom was in the laundry room folding clothes late in the morning, she noticed my food was untouched. She tried calling me to the laundry room, but I just went to the door and refused to go inside. She brought my bowl to the doorway and I started toward the bowl and then

walked away. Now, she was getting concerned. When I still hadn't eaten at noon, I thought I was going to faint from hunger. But if I wanted this to work, I had to see my plan through to fruition. Mom went to the laundry room specifically to see if I'd eaten. When she saw that I had not, she brought the bowl to me in the hallway where I lay next to Lucy's bathroom. She bent down and placed the bowl in front of me. Just a few more feet Mom, but not just yet. I moved into the bathroom and lay on the shag throw rug. By this time, she was totally confused and I could tell that she was beginning to worry. I certainly didn't want her to worry so much that she took me to the vet, but I needed a little longer. She was very smart. She'd get it soon. And then she set the food bowl inside the bathroom door and pretended to walk on down the hall. I waited just a couple of seconds and then went to the food bowl and began to eat. Yes, she got it. She peeked around the door and smiled. "Well, I guess since you're sleeping in Lucy's room, there's no point in leaving all of your things in the laundry room. I think it would be OK to bring your food and water in here. Maybe we can even give Lucy the responsibility of feeding you now."

Alright, that's two things I can check off my to-do list. Next item – the litter box. I thought about leaving little gifts where I wanted the litter box to be moved, but that could have very negative effects. I've heard of cats getting taken back to the shelter for failure to use the litter box. Finally, I hatched a brilliant plan.

I saw this cat on The Animal Network whose humans had taught him to use *their* litter box – you know the one with the blue water in it? Now, like most cats, I'm not partial to water and the thought of possibly losing my footing and falling into cold, blue water is frightening, but if I could pull it off, there would be no need for the litter box at all. It was worth a shot. I am, after all, of superior intelligence. If some run-of-the-mill cat can do it, I'm sure I can. I'm off to give it a try.

If I may digress for a moment, while we're discussing The Animal Network, I feel the need to share what I've learned with all you cat owners out there. You see, Mom leaves the TV on for me when the family's gone for any length of time because she thinks I'll get lonely. Sweet sentiment, but I really could use the peace and quiet. At any rate, I'm sure she has no idea the kinds of things they show on that channel or she would realize that allowing me to watch it would certainly do nothing toward helping me to relax. I thought I'd had a rough life before coming here, but the things I see animals have to endure on some of those shows is beyond what you'd call abuse. They say a lot of the animals come into the shelter having been purposely burned and otherwise tortured by their owners. Other are merely neglected without food or water or shelter and left to die a sad and painful death. They say that by donating money to the shelters and animal control facilities, you can help to stop this from happening and I'd sure appreciate it if you'd give that some thought.

Now, moving on to my adventure with the human's maniacal plumbing fixture. Being a little girl's toilet, the seat was down and the lid was up. That was a plus, because my lack of opposable thumbs is really a hindrance. The toilets in the rest of the house have blue water in them. I personally have never seen water that blue, but it certainly makes more sense than the pink water in Lucy's toilet. I can't even fathom how one turns water pink. So, I climb on the ledge between the seat and the tank. There were two large bolts which I assumed hold the seat in place. Excellent. Bolts that big should make this contraption extremely secure, I surmised. Now how did that cat on TV position himself? Let's see, I would need my front paws to balance up in the front of the hole and then one back leg on the other side of the hole and the other leg... *oh sweet Heaven*!

I struggled in the icy cold water for what seemed to be an eternity. The porcelain was slick. If only they had spent a little more money for one of those padded seats like I saw at Vinnie's, then I could've sunk my claws in and pulled my way up. And Vinnie's special toilet had been heated and it— oh no! What if this was one of those self-flushing models? I could be washed out to the East River and never seen again. Even worse, I'd heard that there are alligators the size of eighteen wheelers in the sewers of New York. What a ghastly way to die. There would be no trace of me. I would just vanish, never to be seen again. Just as my pink body began to

lose all feeling from the frigid water, I heard Lucy screaming for her mother. She had come home from school and found me drowning in her toilet. Help was on the way!

Mom arrived just in time to rescue me from my horrid pink nightmare. She took me into the laundry room and put me in the deep utility sink and scrubbed me with that blue dishwashing liquid that they use on ducks when they rescue them from an oil spill. Unfortunately, it didn't do much towards removing pink dye. Now I really couldn't go out of the house. Big tough mobster with pink hair. The boys would never let me live that one down. And for an added bonus – the pink water was lavender scented. What *was* it with this woman and the scent of lavender?

After I endured twenty minutes of blow drying, I went to Lucy's room and climbed into my own little bed, which had been positioned near the heat vent, so that I wouldn't catch my death from being chilled to the bone. When I woke, I heard the family at the dinner table and headed down to see what was on the menu. I guess Mom was also tired from my ordeal, as they'd ordered Chinese take-out. Maybe there would be Moo-shoo Pork; that's my favorite. Mom knows it's my favorite, so she had already fixed a little bowl of pork for me and put it near her chair on the floor. When I sat down next to her to eat, she leaned over and stroked my pink fur and told me how sorry she was for my accident and that she thought I was such a smart cat for trying to mimic my humans.

As I readily accepted the 3Ps – praise, pity and pork, I heard a familiar sound outside. I'd completely forgotten about the long Palladian windows in the dining room. They went from ceiling to floor, so I was completely visible to the outside where Johnny stood clawing at the window. The annoying scratching did not go unnoticed. Dad stood and threw his napkin on the table and headed for the front door. Mom told him it was probably just one of my friends wanting me to come out and play. Ha! Yeah, you might call it that. Dad said he didn't care what the mangy beast wanted. *He* wanted to eat his meal in peace and quiet. Dad had caught Johnny scratching at the laundry room window before. He had shredded the screen so badly that it had to be replaced. There were no screens on the formal windows in the dining room, so he was not going to allow the filthy animal to scratch the glass!

Johnny is as loyal to Vinnie as the day is long. He would carry a message by foot in a thunder storm all the way to California if Vinnie asked him to. He wouldn't rest until the message had been delivered, even if it meant me getting sent back up the ladder to personal assistant to Van Gato; so he was not deterred by Dad shouting obscenities. He kept signalling me to come outside. I just looked innocently at Mom as though I had no idea what was wrong with the poor misguided feline. Dad pulled out the big guns – the garden hose. He nearly drowned Johnny, but Johnny stood his ground, even though he was drenched to the hide and water was snorting from his nostrils. He never wavered. If I ever have the opportunity (and by now, I was suspecting that would be sooner rather than later), I would tell Vinnie what a faithful and loyal member of his organization Johnny is. Let him go ahead and take my position on the roster. I wanted out anyway.

The more Johnny resisted Dad's threats, the angrier and more determined Dad became. When he came inside to get his BB gun, I had to do something. After all, Johnny wasn't the one who had led me along this path of self-destruction; nor had Vinnie for that matter. I had no one to blame but myself and I was the only one who could turn my life around. I ran out the pet door and Johnny and I made a quick get-away before Dad found his ammunition.

We didn't stop for a breath until we reached Flushing Avenue. By then, Johnny was shivering uncontrollably from both the unexpected shower and fear. It was my turn to pay it forward. I shared with him a little trick that Goo and I had perfected during our winters in Philly.

"Johnny, I don't know why I care that you're cold and wet and might catch your death. I guess you think I don't know that you've been trying for months to discredit me in Vinnie's eyes in order to regain your place in the organization." Johnny started to deny my allegations, but I held up my paw and stopped him. "Don't try to deny it. I know exactly what you've said behind my back and ya know what, Johnny? I don't care. I don't care what happens to me. I hate what I've become and someway, somehow, I'm going to turn my life around." I'd probably said too much, but I really didn't care about any of it anymore. Let him go running to Vinnie. It would just save me the trouble. I grabbed the scruffy little weasel by the neck and shoved him into the public restroom.

"Now just shut up Johnny and do what I tell you. This is something my brother Goo and I learned when we were on the streets. When the temperatures dropped below zero, which they often did, we would sneak into the public restrooms and I would jump on top of the hand dryer and push the big silver button while Goo stood below the nozzle and warmed himself. To this day, I don't know how Goo was able to estimate the height of an object and jump up onto it, but he seldom missed or lost his footing. When he was warm, he would tell me to jump down and he'd get up on the dryer and press the button a few times for me. Now stand right below the nozzle and I'll push the button,"

Johnny agreed that was a great idea, so he did as he was told while I assisted in blow drying his matted fur. I think maybe that single act of kindness might have softened Johnny's view of me, at least temporarily, but you just never could tell with Johnny what was going on in his twisted mind.

On the walk to Manhattan, Johnny told me that Vinnie had actually come to Brooklyn looking for me himself the day before. I asked if he was angry but Johnny said that he seemed genuinely worried about me. He told some of the guys that he was afraid maybe I'd been in an accident – maybe even killed by a car or any of a thousand other things that can (and do) happen to an animal on the streets. I was touched by Vinnie's concern, but I could not appear vulnerable in any manner when I talked to Vinnie. I had resolved to lay it all on the table and hand in my resignation once and for all.

Although I knew that Johnny had thrown me under the bus on more than one occasion, due to jealousy. I hoped that was telling the truth about Vinnie's concern for my well-being. But apparently, the time for trusting Johnny as an ally and friend was over. Vinnie did not greet me with the joy of a father welcoming home the prodigal son. He merely gave me the once-over and without so much as a hello, went to pour himself a nice bowl of chilled Bling H_2O, which he lapped down, never once offering to share with Johnny or me. Afterward, he lay back on his kitty-king bed and washed his whiskers as he finally began to speak.

"So, been havin' yerself a vacation or what, kid? You know it's only polite to check in wich yer employer ever once in a while – that is, if youse expect to keep yer job,"

And there was my opening. "Well, you see Vinnie, that's just it. I ran into my brother – you know, the one who is blind – the other day and, well, it got me to thinking. We were catching up and he was telling me what all he's done since we saw each other. He was actually in town for a photo shoot for a magazine! He's going to be on the cover of the next edition. He told me that he'd met a real nice girl and they had three boys back in Philly. He's been adopted by some real nice people over in Jersey. I mean, as I was listening to what all Goo's managed to make of his life, well it made me stop and think *what have I really done with my life*?"

Vinnie seemed to listen intently to what I was saying, without comment. He didn't appear flustered or perturbed, so I went in for the kill.

"So you see, Vinnie, I need to make a change in my life and do something significant; something that when I'm dead and gone, people will say 'He mattered. He made an impact.' That's why I'm just not going to be able to do any more jobs for you. You understand, don't you Vinnie?"

Very calmly and matter-of-factly, Vinnie turned away from me and looked out onto Central Park. Then he turned around and laughed a maniacal laugh. "Johnny's been watching you for weeks now, Punk. He reports that you've been hiding out from me. Is that true, Punk?" Vinnie was now punching me in the chest with every staccato syllable of his words. "I believe I made it perfectly clear on numerous occasions that this is a lifetime position. You don't just up and quit the organization, Frankie. If yas was to quit and go off on yer own, you might – completely unintentionally, I'm sure – tell somebody something just innocent-like that could cause the rest of us a whole lot of grief." At this point,

Vinnie began to slap my cheeks. "Now youse wouldn't wanna hurt all yer brothers and me, would ya, Frankie? Now go on outta here and let me sleep off this headache that you've given me and we'll never speak of this again. Do you understand?"

"But Vinnie, I owe it to my family to go straight and to do something worthwhile," I said. "I'm not going to change my mind. I've decided and that's that."

That did it. That pushed the launch sequence button. His tail and his whiskers began to twitch and the fur on his back stood up as though he was about to attack. His eyes glowed orange, as they had the first day we met. He hissed and I swear I saw venom spray from his long canine teeth. Then, just as suddenly as his violent temper had erupted, his features relaxed and he became amazingly calm.

"Yeah. OK. Well, I see that you're a man of conviction, Frankie. You go on now and I hope that you find your dream. Good luck to you." And with that, he extended his paw in friendship and one last time, he patted me on the back.

I heaved a sigh of relief and walked towards

the elevator. As I stood waiting for the car to arrive, Vinnie fired a parting shot, which I should've known was coming.

"Oh and Frankie... I wouldn't get too comfy in yer little family cottage. Things can change in the blink of any eye, ya know. You might wanna sleep wit one eye open." With that, he chuckled under his breath and walked out onto the balcony overlooking the park, leaving me to wonder what I had just done.

While I know that Vinnie is at least twenty per cent hot air I also know that he had ordered his men (as well as contacts throughout the East Coast) to perform some truly unspeakable acts against anyone who dared to cross him. The general rule of thumb in any organization is:

1) never 'wrong' any member of the organization and

2) never, ever insult or humiliate the leader of the organization.

I had just broken both cardinal rules. I had 'wronged' Vinnie as well as insulting and humiliating him. To allow me to just walk away would cause him to lose face with all of his friends and associates, and more importantly, his enemies. Even if he wanted to, he couldn't allow me to leave unscathed. I needed to run away. Somewhere far away. Somewhere that no one would ever find me.

I went back home and tried to hatch a plan, but I didn't like the idea of running away and leaving the family wondering what had happened to me and whether I was dead or alive. Poor Goo had wondered all this time if I had survived. That's another thing... I just found my little brother again. He wasn't too far away and I didn't want to lose touch ever again. I could head back to Philly and meet Olivia and Abigail and my three nephews. Then maybe someday when things had time to blow over, I could come back and visit Goo with a report on his little family. But I might as well stay here and let Vinnie's goons take me out as to go back to Philly and let Snake and the Brawlers have the pleasure of finishing the job. No, I would just stay here and face up to the mess I've made of my life. If I'm to pay the ultimate price for my poor decisions, then so be it. Maybe I'll luck out and Vinnie will decide I'm not worth his trouble.

A Light Through Yonder Window Breaks

I took the shortcuts and back roads all the way home. I never stopped looking over my shoulder because I felt as though Vinnie's parting words were still hanging over my head like thick, syrupy fog everywhere I went. When I finally reached our house without incident, I knew that I was living on borrowed time and it wouldn't be long until I found out just how far I had pushed the envelope and had no idea what form Vinnie's vengeance would take. I had to come up with a plan, and fast. It needed to be something that wouldn't hurt my family, so I couldn't run away, but maybe just an extended vacation. But I couldn't explain that to the family either. They'd grown accustomed to me being gone a few days here and there, but weeks and months? Out of the question.

I hated to admit it, but I needed protection. Well, that wasn't going to happen either. I'd been too busy associating with the wrong class of cats to make any real or lasting friendships. The only cat I trusted with my life was Goo and he couldn't help. Maybe I could show up at his place in Brooklyn and his family would adopt me too. No, I'd already spilled Goo's name and whereabouts to Vinnie. He'd find us and I wasn't about to put Goo in danger.

I couldn't think in the confines of the house. I had to walk it off. Although I was shaking like a leaf and terrified of who or what might be lurking outside in wait, I had to get some fresh air and think.

Protection... someone to protect me from Vinnie and everyone associated with him. It had to be someone who was near enough that I didn't have to leave home, and someone who was untouchable.

As I paced around and around the yard, I suddenly noticed a flash of light. I hit the ground and covered my head, envisioning that the flash had come from a gunshot or a Molotov cocktail or grenade. I didn't know what might be in store for me. When the light didn't dissipate, nor was it accompanied by a loud bang, I dared to peek out from beneath my arm. The light was coming from next door. Giselle had switched on the back porch light. That was our signal that she wanted some company. I ran and quickly scooted beneath the stairs and up through the hole in the floor. Giselle was standing at the top of the hole giggling.

"What kind of crazy game are you up to now, Frank?" she asked. "You looked so silly out there, like a baseball player sliding into home base, holding onto his cap."

"Trust me, Giselle, this is no game I'm playing," I said. "I'm in big trouble and I don't know what to do or where to turn."

Giselle put her paw on my back and gently rubbed against my whiskers with her head

"Frank, you should know by now that you certainly have one friend that you can trust implicitly. Why, I know what you're going to say most times before you say it. We finish each other's sentences a lot of times, have you noticed that? I knew the path you would choose before you chose it. From the day you first asked me about Vincent Van Gato, I knew that you were destined to fall under his spell. It wasn't so much what you said as what you didn't say," Giselle told me.

"I know that you didn't get to have a childhood, darling Frank. You had appointed yourself poor little Goo's guardian, sweet boy that you are. I knew that you would get restless as a mere housecat. I knew that you would have to go seeking adventure and nothing I said would've changed that wanderlust. You had to learn life's lessons for yourself. I've been praying that you would eventually make the right decisions and extricate yourself from Vinnie's grip before you ended up as Nicky did. I didn't want you to also have a life cut short and without meaning." I reached over and put my arm across her shoulders.

For so long, I've told myself that I have no friends, when all along, the best friend anyone could ask for was sitting right in the next sunbeam waiting and praying for me to come home, my sweet Giselle.

I thought she'd almost said that she loves me once before and if I'd ever had any doubts about my feelings for her there was no longer any question. But I had to sort out my life before I could offer to share it with anyone else. I just prayed that I would be given the time.

THE RECKONING

Fall came early to New York this year. Since Lucy has started school, Mom took a part-time job, so I've been alone most days until late afternoon.

Every day was becoming an endless rotation of sleeping and eating. When eating is your only form of exercise, you pack on the pounds rapidly and your metabolism slows down so that sleeping is about all you can muster the energy to do, and so it was with me.

Having been active all of my life, I didn't like the way I was feeling and looking, so I did what I knew I had to do – I exercised. I did what I could within the confines of my house. I became a runner. I ran up and down the steps. I ran up and down the halls. I ran in circles around every room in the house. Problem was, I had been used to sleeping all day and working all night, so when I would get the urge to exercise after everyone else in the household went to sleep at night, they weren't exactly thrilled. I tried to turn it all around and do my exercise regime during the day and sleep when the family slept at night, but it just wasn't working for me.

Since there have been no attempts by Vinnie or any of the boys to contact me in weeks, I determined that it would be okay to go outside at night and exercise in my own yard. It's worked out fine until just recently. I would do laps around the yard, climb a tree or two and then jump the fence back and forth a few times. I could really tell a difference in my stamina and I was once again looking like a lean, mean, fighting machine. Of course, with increased stamina comes a higher metabolism and I began to sleep less and want to run around at night more and more, so I expanded my jogging trail. I ran over to Giselle's yard. She also sleeps more during the day and was awake all night, so sometimes she comes out and joins me for a jog.

I guess I didn't realize that there were so many normal cats that are nocturnal. By 'normal', I mean those not involved in organized crime activity.

Giselle has introduced me to a great group of housecats right on our own street and we've formed our own little exercise group that we call The Night Owls. It's good, clean, healthy fun, and getting healthy has made me feel good about myself.

🐈 🐈 🐈

I've put aside my fears of retribution from Vinnie and allowed my perimeters to expand further and further with my new friends, the Night Owls. Fuelled by the adrenaline to which we have both become addicted, Giselle and I have decided to challenge the rest of the Night Owls to a five kilometer run. We've had fun mapping out the route for the race.

My brain has been so much in overdrive that danger never crossed my mind. We've put the finish line on the Brooklyn Bridge. This was the very bridge on which I had received the rites of induction into the Van Gato organization, but all thoughts of my former, shady life have vanished for the moment, as my confidence about my future overshadows my past.

I owe the new Frank to Giselle. She has revitalized not only my physical and mental health, but she brings out the best in me. I want to the best I can be for her. I love Giselle and she has shown me is so many ways that she feels the same about me. When we reach the finish line tonight, I'm going to ask her to spend the rest of her life with me, so I can try to make her as happy as she's made me.

The Night Owls assembled on Cook Street, where this afternoon, Giselle and I drew a line across the road with sidewalk chalk that I borrowed from Lucy's backpack. And now, we all stood with our front paws on the line, waiting for the sound of the 1:45 train whistle to signal our start.

On your mark...

Get set...

Go!

I was so focused on the finish line and the ultimate prize (when I ask Giselle to be my life mate), that I was virtually flying through the course. I've slowed down only once. That was when I realized that my plans would be for naught if I beat Giselle to the finish, so I let her catch up to me. We finished a good three minutes before any of the other Night Owls.

We sat down on the curb beside the walkway to catch our breath when we realized that weren't alone.

We were surrounded by Vinnie and his gang of outlaws. I tried to shield Giselle by stepping in between her and Vinnie.

"What's a matter, pretty boy?" asked Vinnie. "Don't you look fine with your new muscular physique. And who's dat pretty little thing you're trying to hide from me? You done gone and got yerself a galfriend, pretty boy? Hmmm?" He smirked at me. "Well, pity she's going to have to see you *die*." Vinnie turned to his hoods. "Go on boys, it's time this traitor takes a nice dip in the river. And don't forget to put the pretty necklace we brought for him around his neck,"

"With pleasure," says Johnny as he steps forward brandishing a heavy gold chain which Vinnie had stolen from the Missus. He began to wrap it around my neck, all the way down to and around my forelegs.

The weight of the chains made me sink to the pavement. Vinnie gave the signal for the boys to toss me over the bridge's railing. They formed a pyramid to begin dragging my body up and over the iron bars.

Suddenly, Giselle breaks between the boys and the railing and screams. "Van Gato, give the order to put him down. NOW!"

Vinnie ordered the boys to halt long enough for him to hear her out.

"Awww... are you sad you're going to lose your little boyfriend?" Vinnie laughs. "Well, you're a pretty little thing. I might just have to take you home with me. I bet you'd forget all about this loser if you was to live in a Park Avenue penthouse, wouldn't you little Miss... what's yer name sweetheart? I don't believe we've been properly introduced."

"You know me, you slimy bastard," she sad. "I'm Giselle." Seeing no sign of recognition from Vinnie, she continued, "You killed my brother, Nicolai"

Again, Vinnie shook his head and shrugged his shoulders.

"Nicky. You killed Nicky," Giselle said.

With that, Vinnie realizes who she is and motions for the boys to put me down.

"Ah yes, Nicky. Such a shame about his accident."

"It was no accident. If you hadn't sucked him into your tangled, despicable little web, it never would have happened. You sent an innocent

boy to do your dirty work, because you're not man enough to take care of business yourself."

I can't believe that meek, mild-mannered little Giselle is standing nose-to-nose with the meanest, deadliest cat in all of the East Coast.

"Now watch yer mouth little girl. I said I was sorry about your loss, but you don't know who you're talking to, Now let's just calm down and talk about this rationally," Vinnie said.

"I do know exactly who and what I'm talking to. I also know that if you don't want to lose face with all of your colleagues, you'll let Frank go free and never bother him again. Your kind may not have any morals or dignity, but you do have a strict code that you never break a promise. Now keep your promise and let Frank go!"

"Honey, I made a promise to you years ago that you would be protected and that no harm would come to you and your family ever again. But what's that got to do with Frankie here? Don't try to tell me he's your long-lost brother because I know everything there is to know about him and his family." Vinnie looked at me.

"Frank *is* my family," Giselle said. "We were just about to have a commitment ceremony before you so rudely interrupted."

I look at Giselle with what I can only imagine is surprise and great joy. But Vinnie isn't buying what she is selling just yet.

"Now how do I know what you're spoon feeding me is true?"he asked.

"Well, if you look over your shoulder, you'll see the rest of our wedding party arriving at this very moment, Vinnie," I said.

As the rest of the Night Owls crossed the invisible finish line, I finished removing the chain from around my neck and set about building our case for clemency.

"We were beginning to wonder if any of you were going to make it to the ceremony." Before anyone could question what I was talking about, I continued and point out my closest tom friend in the group, the one I had told my intentions toward Giselle. I had also felt comfortable enough to talk to him about my past. He took one look around and immediately surmised what was happening and took charge.

"Ok, now if all of you will just gather around Frank and Giselle, we'll get on with our commitment service and then we're off to party and celebrate until dawn. Frank, I assume these are some of your friends from the city" he said, motioning toward Vinnie and his gang.

"Yes. Certainly. You're all welcome to join us in our celebration."

Vinnie has no alternative than to regain his composure and order the boys to quiet down and stand up straight.

With that, I took Giselle's hand and as we stood on the Brooklyn Bridge, looking across at the Manhattan skyline, we looked into each other's eyes and said our vows.

"I, Giselle, take you, Frank, to be my partner for as long as our humans live next door to each other. I will always trust in you and cherish you. I will spend every moment possible by your side."

"I, Frank, take you Giselle to be my partner, understanding that as house pets, we can never be assured that one or both of us might not be moved away to another street, another city, another state or even another country; and while there are no assurances that our owners will love us, take care of us and even keep us until the end of our days, even so, I commit my heart to you for all time."

And so our lives together have begun,

Vinnie's not one to apologize, but he has assured Giselle that he is a man of his word and that should either of us ever be in danger, all we have to do is get word to him and he will protect us. I hope that we never have to call on Vincent Van Gato ever again.

CPSIA information can be obtained at www.ICGtesting.com
Printed in the USA
BVOW01s1143020614

355156BV00001B/1/P

9 780992 333997